Divertimento

Also by Julie Thorndyke and published by Ginninderra Press
Mrs Rickaby's Lullaby

Divertimento

Julie Thorndyke

Divertimento
ISBN 978 1 76109 090 5
Copyright © text Julie Thorndyke 2021
Cover image: *Woman at a Piano*, Pierre August Renoir, imitator of;
The Art Institute of Chicago

First published 2021 by
GINNINDERRA PRESS
PO Box 3461 Port Adelaide 5015
www.ginninderrapress.com.au

Contents

Divertimento

'Got a lovely growl, hasn't it?' The shop manager speaks behind my left shoulder.

I'd been riffing along on an ebony concert grand, getting a little carried away.

I apologise for playing the instrument without first being invited to try it out. To be fair, he was busy with another customer when I came into the music store, otherwise I would have waited. But I'm on my lunch hour, time is precious. Life is measured in minims, crochets, quavers. No time to waste.

'Be my guest,' he schmoozes. Then come the questions: what am I looking for? New or second-hand? Japanese or German? And…do I have a budget in mind?

I've a standard set of answers to these questions in my repertoire. Enough detail to string him along with a believable tune but nothing that will give away my real financial troubles. There are three music shops within walking distance of the office where my time is clocked on and off – I am working my way through all three as the metronome clicks through this week of temporary office work.

'Let me show you this little beauty,' he says, walking ahead, deeper inside the showroom to a European model behind a blue curtain. He slides back the mahogany fallboard, lifts the lid and settles the long prop gently on the felted depression on the underside.

He plays the first bars of a Mozart sonata, then waves an invitation to sit on the faux leather stool and play. I make it my policy not to play well-known pieces in public. I'm not interested in having people notice me, as they might if I played a favourite melody that lingered in the air, resonating in their minds. I just improvise; try a scale or arpeggio; a few bars of my own melodies and some cadences stolen from the master-works. Just enough so that I will be recognised as a seasoned pianist: perhaps an underpaid teacher, or professional accompanist.

I don't feel the same affection for the gleaming varnish of this tawny lion as I did for the sleek black panther that had been purring for me moments ago.

I ask for the manager's card before I leave: a simple demonstration of sincerity that might provide some uninterrupted practice time on a future visit.

Winding my plaid scarf around my neck, I express my thanks and step through the mosaic foyer into the city street. The frigid air bites my fingertips, that had been warmed by the pulsing exercise, but are now chilling rapidly. I plunge my hands into my pockets. Damn. Left my gloves on the edge of the first piano.

I smile upwards into the pearly sky, and taste the falling moisture on my tongue. It's a ready-made reason to return to that black panther as soon as I can.

♬♬♫

Luck is on my side: the phones are silent and the meeting rooms empty. The boss says a swift goodbye as she clicks down the echoing hall on the way to collect her children from day care. I have the desk tidy and the PC ready to log off precisely at five. I am out of the door at 5.01 p.m. A nod to the security guard, wish him a good weekend, and I am away.

Still freezing, there is an energy in the moist air as cars swish along the streets, workers jog for buses, children stomp in puddles. Shoppers stop to look in windows, bouncing on the spot to keep warm. Fairy lights on bare-limbed trees are reflected on the wet streets and a frag-ment of melody rises from a hardy busker sheltering with his violin in a covered lane.

I hope that the music store is open late: the card that my eager fin-gers curl, deep inside my pocket, lists no opening hours. But when I arrive, the doors are firmly shut, a chain and padlock bound around the square handles. Closed for the weekend.

Walking away, rhythms thrumming in my head, idly hoping for some unexpected good fortune to come my way, I thrust my hands deeper into my pockets. I have a coin left, so I seek out the violinist and toss it meekly into his open case. No busking for piano players. There's good luck, the Irish say, in giving away your last coin. The widow's mite. Does it hold true in these days of electronic transactions? I'm willing to hope.

♫♫♫

I've a few ways to feed my habit.

There's a low-cost dance class in a ramshackle church basement run by an elderly teacher who prefers a piano player to recorded twangs. The instrument, if slipping out of tune, is a good solid brown bear of Russian manufacture. I can pick my key and get a good sound out of it. The ballet teacher likes standard classics – the same ones over and over – just a little slower, a tad faster, depending on her mood and how much vodka is left in her water bottle.

I arrive early, stay late, play whatever I like while the children and their mothers mill around, adding or subtracting layers of clothing, changing shoes. The old dame pays me a pittance, which I spend on a meal afterwards.

From this contact came a query from a choir, could I accompany? They'd heard about my cheap rates. That turned out to be gold: a nicely tuned concert grand in a private school hall. They have to throw me out of that venue. Otherwise, the student practice rooms at the conservatorium are my haunt. Not during exam weeks. People know me there, but don't challenge my presence.

These are the ways I keep my ear tuned, my fingers limber. My hope alive.

♫♫♫

There's a woman hunched over her clicking knitting needles, behind the desk of the twenty-four-hour laundry. The machines – the stainless steel washing and drying cubes, soap dispensers, the change machine – are self-service. The woman is there to keep an eye on things. She doesn't have much to do. Mop the floor if there's a spill; chase out a noisy drunk (the quiet ones, she leaves in peace); call the police if thugs begin trashing the place. That's why she's on duty: people can't be trusted not to vandalise an unsupervised shop. I don't know if she's here in the daytime, I only wash on Saturday night.

The caretaker-woman knits, clicking over the minutes in a steady waltz rhythm. I've never seen her use a pattern: her unique symphonies of texture and tone are executed from memory or improvisation. Beanies in rib and moss stich; scarves in rainbow stripes of garter stitch finished off with tassels; multi-hued shawls to rival Joseph's famed coat. With a ballpoint pen, she writes modest prices on torn squares of scrap paper, pins these meagre labels to the finished garments and pegs each masterpiece to a festive string that garlands her sanctum near the front door.

Sometimes on a frigid night, a tourist will buy a beanie to warm their skull before venturing out into the winter wind. Other times, I've seen the woman retrieve a just-finished scarf from under the bench and wrap it tenderly around an old man's wrinkled, bent neck. He recognises his team colours and beams with pleasure. She knows all the regulars.

How do I know so much about this place? It isn't a bad retreat to sit with a book, and doze to the crescendo and diminuendo of the washers. There's a vending machine, and if coins have been left behind in the drop, a chocolate bar might be subsidised. The woman doesn't bother with such things, but won't tolerate any percussion on the vending machine for freebies.

While my two sets of grimy clothes and one bath towel take a slow allemande in the washer, I wait in comfort throughout the night. Safer than riding trains and buses. Warmer than the park. Less dangerous than public conveniences. The other good places are all-night university study halls. The staff are so used to seeing me there with my piles of scores and manuscript pages, pencilling crotchets and quavers and rubbing them out again, that they never ask for ID or notice that I ceased being a bona fide student long ago. Once or twice, the librarians in the main building have missed checking the toilets at closing time. Their staffroom, with bench seats to lie on, free tea and coffee, makes quite a reasonable night's lodging.

If you don't look like a homeless person, some inner-city churches are warm and their music a pleasant diversion on a Sunday evening. There's often a hot drink and a snack on offer. Be elusive about your profession and residence, don't return too often, and it will work out fine. Gyms and swimming pools are good if you can gain access. Hot showers and free shampoo, hairdryers. There's a restaurant in Chinatown, worth the detour, that lets me wash dishes for a free meal. It all helps.

On this night, the woman behind the laundromat desk reaches into her plastic bag of higgledy-piggledy yarn scraps, retrieves a soft bundle and places it on my chilly palm. Soft, grey, fingerless mittens with a crimson Fair Isle pattern around the ribbed wrists. How could she know that the practice rooms are unheated and scarcely bearable in winter?

I offer the woman a gold coin, one of three I found in the vending machine.

She pushes it back across the grey Laminex counter. 'A gift,' she says. 'From one insomniac to another.'

I pull the mittens over my knuckles onto my muscular, thickly veined hands. No denying it, the hands of a pianist are unmistakable. I bow my silent thanks. Heading out into the cold, my clean clothes folded neatly in my backpack, pressed between piano scores, I wonder, what have I let slip? Is it my hair: too unkempt? My clothes: too worn and creased? My shoes: out-dated and inappropriate? I don't believe that I emit any unpleasant odour, but maybe I'm wrong.

Perhaps she's seen the way I handle money, one coin at a time, careful beyond normal limits. My miserly use of soap powder? The way I always check the snack machine for change? No, any thrifty person might do that. My slow departure? I must have succumbed to that uncertain demeanour, that lack of trust and expectation, that distinguishes the urban nomad.

I reject the word homeless. I have a postal address, and a place where things that belong to me are stored in cardboard boxes. Certificates. Photographs. Books and music scores. All in a triangular, piano-shaped room.

To return to that place is both depressing and risky. I try to come and go invisibly. Too much is made of my furtive arrivals and departures, too much blame and shame apportioned to each visit. But tonight, emboldened by kindness and wearing my new mittens, I walk to the bus stop, wait for the familiar numerals on the forehead of the chugging bus, climb aboard and pay the fare.

It's late, and the windows are dark, when I step through the gateway to the small garden graced by a single magnolia tree, and head down the side of the two-storey Victorian villa. I unlock the door of the studio quietly. In summer, Gavin is likely to be away, but in winter he lives in the house, teaching in the front music room, watched by the portrait of his dead opera singer mother. Like his father, composer Simon Morris, Gavin is a musician.

I was an international student on a scholarship when Gavin's mother died. I had won the famed piano competition, and for a while was the next big thing. I studied composition with Simon, and became involved with my teacher, enacting that old cliché of older man and adoring protégée. I moved into the house as Simon's lover, Gavin's babysitter and all-purpose cook. After supervising Gavin's breakfast and walking him to school, I would tread quietly upstairs to Simon's bedroom where, inevitably, he was snoring. He kept artist's hours: awake all night, composing, reading, cursing... You could hear him even in my attic bedroom. We didn't share the master. His wife's presence was still everywhere in evidence. Her china figurines on the mantelpiece, her chintz curtains on the tall windows, her fur coats in the closet. Each morning I entered the sanctum, removed my clothes, and slid beneath the doona, resting my cool skin against Simon's overheated body, until he roused, hungry for lovemaking and ravenous for breakfast.

Simon and I never married. There was no need. I had permanent residency, and our life was settled and calm. Fourteen years we lived, the three of us, in domestic harmony. The only quarrel was about the piano, all of us needing to practice, and only one instrument in the house. So, my dear Simon bought a shiny black grand for my birthday, installing it in the converted outbuilding that was to be my studio. Then he died.

Gavin tried to charge me rent. One day when I was out, all of my belongings were moved into the studio. He changed the locks on the house. The little boy I had soothed with cuddles and bedtime stories had morphed into the wicked stepson. I had no legal relationship. No proof of his father's commitment. On paper, I sounded like a live-in housekeeper, not a de facto wife. Legally I could make a claim for the house I had shared for more than a decade.

Gavin disagreed. 'Be grateful I let you live in the studio,' he said. 'Most people would throw you out on the street.'

My career had never really taken off. I hadn't completed my qualifications, believing that I would always be safe beneath Simon's protective wing. I tried teaching, but Gavin didn't like the disruption of my students in the house. My scholarship was long gone and my postgrad student debt unpaid.

The air in the small studio is colder than the air outside. No heating. I fill the kettle and plug it in, but sit in the dark. There's no kitchen, just a small sink with a cold water tap. No bathroom, just a toilet in a concrete-floored room that was once the garden shed. I used to sneak into the house for a shower, after Gavin had changed the locks. Until he threatened me.

Drunk, he strode into the bathroom as I stood under the steaming water, looking my naked body up and down. 'I don't know why dear papa bothered with you,' he sneered. 'Cheap labour, I guess. You weren't much of a cook. Guess you had other ways of…pleasing him. Diverting him from grief.'

This malicious streak must have come from his mother. By all accounts, she'd been an ambitious, manipulative overachiever. Her son, once a vulnerable and needy child, had become my enemy.

There's a sofa, bookshelves and piles of my things in packing boxes in the corner. Dominating the room, my piano. In my mind's eye, that is. I snap on the light. All that remains of my shiny black grand are three deep indents impressed in the grey carpet.

'What piano?' Gavin had asked, when challenged. 'The rental? The company reclaimed it.'

'It wasn't a rental, and you know it,' I had replied, standing my ground. 'It was a gift.'

'You're living in a fairy tale,' Gavin retorted. 'Find yourself another Prince Charming to keep you, Cinderella.'

I sip hot black tea. My hands, still in the mittens, are the warmest part of me.

I turn out the light and curl up on the sofa to sleep. Each time I come back, I wonder if my key will fit the lock, whether my belongs will still be here. I have three hundred dollars in my bank account from the temporary job. I'll need to top that up very soon.

Still no lights in the house. What would Gavin do if I simply broke in, locked myself in the attic bedroom and refused to leave?

I doze off, planning the coming day: an appointment to thump out tunes for baby ballet; an afternoon concert in a church hall where there'll be a spread of cakes for afternoon tea. Living hand-to-mouth takes forethought.

I wake, after midnight, aware of music drifting from the house. Without thinking, I toss aside the blanket and head across the courtyard. There is a yellow gleam from upstairs, and the back door is unlocked. Gavin doesn't know I am on the property. The music isn't from the piano. It's a coloratura soprano in full flight. I move through the house, dodging empty beer bottles, tiptoeing up the stairs, following the sound. Gavin is on the landing, standing at the open French doors behind a Juliet balcony, absorbed in the recorded voice of his mother. The volume is fortissimo, he doesn't hear my footsteps. He leans out over the balcony, beer in one hand, the other extended as if to touch the early-blooming magnolia tree. The wrought-iron balcony gives way. Police will discover that the brackets were rusted through, that the smallest weight would have dislodged them.

It's clear – Gavin's crumpled body on the ground has no life within it. This is what I tell myself, as I carry my boxes of belongings from the backyard studio to the master bedroom, remove the figurines and rearrange the room, making it look as if I'd lived there the entire time. Then I phone the ambulance.

Hours later, as I drift into sleep, snug in Simon's large bed, my mind is full of melodies, con brio, that I long to play and transcribe. My gloves are still on the sleek black instrument in the city music shop. I'll go back tomorrow and order that ebony panther. There's Simon's piano downstairs, but it reeks of beer and treachery.

I need to tame a wild piano that will purr, just for me.

Coin of the Crone

Seeing too much is an unwanted gift. Bad enough to be able to sense danger. To be able to see it in full horror, even worse. My visions, vivid and tormenting, were unavoidable. They woke me from sleep, intruded into my self-induced drunken stupors, and burned with fierce intensity into my everyday existence.

I couldn't live a normal life. Sometimes the visions concerned people I had known in childhood before plague took my family from me. Sometimes I saw strangers caught in flames, crushed by earthquake-toppled towers or lost at sea. More often, I didn't know the faces. It was never my own tragedy: my misfortunes came unseen.

In desperation, driven out, I sought solitude in the forest. If I wasn't with people, one of them, I had no obligation to warn of danger. Knowing but not reacting, observing but taking no role. In this way, I would save my body, if not my mind. I could let the drama roll on, keep aloof and let my sensibilities deaden like a well-trodden, dry clay path.

It was a hovel I dwelt in – it couldn't be described as anything else – no glass in the window, just an open gap between rough-hewn timber planks. On an ordinary day, I rubbed my sleep-creased cheek and looked out. The forest was dressed in a petticoat of mist, dispersing even as I watched. It would clear to a fine day. The smell of ash from my cooking fire mingled with the ferny smell of dew-moistened undergrowth. Something rustled – rabbit or fox? I saw nothing. Seeing nothing was a good day.

In a nest fashioned from my one warm cloak and other assorted rags, the baby stirred. One week old, and still a stranger, yet my body responded to his whimper.

He was the child of rape. I had given birth alone in my forest hut, not sure I would let it live. It wouldn't have been the first tiny skeleton

to be found under a tree in the deep recesses of the forest. But his unblinking eyes had met mine as I wiped away the blood from his forehead, demanding protection, so I put him to my breast and he suckled.
He understood more than I.

It had been a holy day when they did it – I'd been keeping myself to
myself a little distance from the hostelry fire. A vision came on, I couldn't
stop it, must have rolled my eyes and passed into a trance: people noticed.
They slapped me, and harassed me until I said what I had seen. I had sworn
not to tell what I saw, ever. It always brings blame. I broke my rule. I saw
the dead child of the tavern keeper on bloodstained sheets, the dead
mother too. As I spoke, the mother's dying screams were heard in the room
above. Of course, they blamed me. It made them feel better to batter my
innocent body. To punish me for witchery, to scorch hair from my head,
to debase a woman, whose mysteries they could not understand.

I paid the price.

I could barely look after myself, but it came to me, like a remembered story, that infants should be fed and washed and rocked to sleep.
I had little food. It hadn't mattered to me whether I starved. But now,
nursing the little son I hadn't intended to keep, I was ravenous. I wandered further from my hut, the child in a sling, to forage for food.

I went to scavenge in an orchard. I laid the child at the base of an
apple tree and gathered windfalls into my shawl. That was when I met
the crone.

The sight of her sent me into a vision, the first since the birth. The
unwanted gift of sight that had plagued me since childhood was still
my master. There was no escaping it.

The crone watched me fade in and out of consciousness. When I
came to, she was sitting on a fallen log cleaning her long grey fingernails.
'You suffer,' she said. 'I can help you.'

'No one can help me.'

'Oh yes, there's a way…but there is always a price.' The crone
scratched her chin and shifted her weight from one buttock to another.
'Sell me the child.'

'The child?'

The crone pushed back the black shawl that covered her head to reveal loose plaits wound around her skull. 'Sell the child and your sight will leave you.'

'How? Why should I believe…'

'That tree,' the old woman pointed at a gnarled oak, larger than any other. 'What do you see?'

I looked, and saw a face carved into the bark. As I watched, flames circled the outline of the face, charring deeper lines into the trunk, leaping like wild tendrils of hair into the air. It was no vision. It was real.

The crone took a gold coin from her pocket. 'Here.' She placed it in my palm. 'You must take the money. I won't eat him!' she laughed. 'Sell the child and you will be free.'

I looked at the round gleam of gold, etched with runes, in my palm. I felt heaviness in my breasts, the drip of milk ready for the babe. I looked up, intending to hand the coin back, but both crone and child were gone.

I slept. Deep, dreamless sleep. Long, empty days. No visions troubled me. My hair grew long and my mind cleared. I left my freezing hut and trudged east, found a village where I was unknown, and work as maidservant to a tailor. He was a childless bachelor who required cooking, cleaning and asked no questions.

Above the village was a knoll with a ruined pagan temple. Only a pile of stones remained, forming a tower supporting an ancient brass bell. The bell seemed familiar, the runes carved into the dull metal pleasing to my eye. It was never rung except as a warning. The village had known many troubles, invaders from the north and pirates from the sea. I went to the knoll on clear days, and looked out into the swirling water. I wondered about the babe and the crone, but so much of my past life was a burden, I learned to lock my thoughts away and live only in the present. I still had the crone's gold coin. It hung in a pouch against my breast. I couldn't bring myself to use it. There was nothing I wished to buy.

As time went on, the tailor became used to my compliant ways and married me. Decades older than I, he asked nothing more than warmth for his cold bed. When he passed from this life in his seventieth year, the cottage became mine and my future seemed secure.

Who can say why then, on this wintry afternoon, I take a much-used candle, and with a knife too sharp for comfort, hollow out the melted wax around the blackened wick?

Perhaps it is a need for extra light in this sunless room – perhaps, although the lamp is full of oil and the fire in the grate crackles willingly enough. Perhaps it is the silence – all noises deadened by the deep blanket of snow – perhaps.

Without pausing for thought, like a mechanical doll, I place the rough cylinder of beeswax on a brass tray. I tug the faded damask curtains to close out the sleety afternoon, and latch the cottage door.

Taking a flaming taper from the fire, I begin to hum, light the wick and with a quick flick of my straight arm cast the taper back into the fire. Squinting until my vision is centred on the single flame, my humming becomes a chant, and I take the crone's gold coin from the pouch that has hung around my neck all these years.

The fire gleams on the coin, and I will my gift of sight to return. After decades apart, I want to know. I want to see my son. I hold the coin over the flame.

When it comes, the vision begins softly, then crescendos into a fierce tide. I see the knoll and the great bell, a tall man ringing it, his unblinking eyes staring into mine. He is sounding the alarm, and as it gets louder in my mind I become aware that it also comes across the snow-covered land, through the village streets to echo around my cottage. The alarm is being sounded, not only in my vision.

I see raiders in long boats land on the pebbled beach, scale the cliffs and swarm through farms and villages with lit torches, brandishing swords. My son rings the bell. I hear the crackle of flame in the thatch of the roof above me. I hear the laugh of the crone, the toll of the bell.

Still holding the searing coin, I close my eyes and wait for the flames to claim me.

The Maid's Room

'Aren't you afraid of Aunt Maud's ghost?' Athena stood in the bedroom doorway, stroking her swollen, pregnant belly. 'You know she died in here.'

Cassandra looked at her twin with impatience and turned back to the large casement window. She pulled off the last vestiges of the dull, brown wartime tape that had crisscrossed the glass. She pushed open the leaded window frames as far as the stiff hinges would permit. 'Fly free, Auntie Maud,' she cried into the brisk autumn wind.

Between their house and the red-brick gabled property next door, a large oak stood, shedding flurries of russet leaves into the stiff breeze. From the window, she could see down the quiet village street, unaltered for decades. There was a hint of wood smoke on the wind. It was 1948 and change was in the air.

'I'm not scared of Auntie,' she said. 'All she ever did was give us barley sugars and sing nursery rhymes.'

'No doubt, she sings you a lullaby every night.'

'While you lie radiantly in your husband's arms!'

'Puke in the lav, more like. This romantic life isn't all it's cracked up to be, sis.'

'Your choice, dearie. Rock the cradle while I…'

'While you what? Play Florence Nightingale and catch dreaded diseases?' Athena was scathing about Cassandra's choice of nursing as a career. After leaving school, they'd both completed secretarial studies, then changed their minds, and began studying for teaching certificates. Athena met engineering student Robert, and 'fell'. Both twins abandoned their studies like a pair of crows dropping inedible stones. All career plans hastily pushed aside, Athena and Robert had wed in a civil service and were installed as a couple in the twins' childhood bedroom. The other large upstairs bedroom across the landing, once the fetid lair of their older twin brothers, was converted for their use as a sitting room.

'You'll want somewhere private of your own,' their mother had said. 'With a sofa and a table and a little gas ring for making supper for two.'

But so far, with cooking smells making Athena nauseous, and a small show of blood causing the doctor to command complete bed rest, all meals were eaten *en famille* downstairs with Cassandra hauling a tray up to her sister's bedroom.

'Better than catching what you caught. Does the doc predict one sprog or two?' asked Cassandra.

'Most likely plural, given the size and family history,' admitted Athena, once more rubbing her belly, prominent beneath her silky apricot nightgown.

Their mother was twin to the late Aunt Maud, who had lived her last spinster years in the little maid's room. For her occupancy, the room had been papered with large blue roses. After several claustrophobic nights staring at these unnatural blooms, Cassandra was in the process of peeling them off. The long, curling streamers of wallpaper were piled on the dust sheeted single bed like an oversized nest of shredded blue feathers. Their parents had been enthusiastic decorators, but frugal with paste. The wallpaper offered no resistance as she tugged and tore layer after layer from the walls. Under the blue rose pattern was a boyish teal design of cowboys and Indians, from a phase when the twin brothers had tried separate rooms. It hadn't lasted. Beneath that, an ivy trellis; below that, rose-coloured stripes. It had been a maid's room once, in the pre-war years when both sets of twins were too young for school and their mother was rushed off her feet and needed live-in help. In the family, it was always known as the maid's room. Recently used for storage, but now cleared of the boxes of Christmas decorations, suitcases and broken toys. A single bed, a wardrobe and a chest of drawers and were in place for Cassandra's use, until she left for the nurses' quarters of the teaching hospital where she had applied to train.

'What paper will *you* have?' asked Athena.

'Just whitewash,' Cassandra said. In her mind's eye, she already had the picture of a clean white room, her neat divan bed covered in a coarse unbleached cotton throw and bright scatter cushions, her new portable record player on the chest of drawers, and a vase of bright zinnias on the windowsill.

'Mother will have this mess covered with new Anaglypta and a pale rose emulsion before you can say –'

'Bollocks,' said Cassandra. She pulled off the last jagged petal of blue rose and rested her aching back on the bare wall. From her pocket, she took a cigarette and lit up.

'Lean out the window, or mother will catch you,' warned Athena.

'Small beer, after *your* transgressions,' said Cassandra.

'Oh! The stink… I'm going to –' Athena rushed to the bathroom.

Cassandra heard her sister retch and vomit. It was enough to warn anyone against physical love for good and all. Was this the way it had been with her mother and Maud? One sister put off marriage by her twin's experience? One thing was for sure, the maid's room was just a temporary bolthole. There was a large wide world out there, waiting for her. She imagined the white walls covered with postcards and pictures sent home from all over the globe.

'For God's sake, get some contraception,' her brothers had advised in a furtive phone call from the army base where they were stationed. 'Don't be as naive as Athena was.'

In an unexpected way, after the initial shouting and shock, their mother had taken Athena's part and done all she could to install the young couple on the upper level of the family home.

Mother had objected loudly when the boys enlisted. 'There's no need!' she had cried. 'The war is over!'

But they went anyway. It was as if she feared empty rooms and the possibility of solitary meals with her silent, work-centred academic husband. Most days, he entered his study in the morning and didn't emerge at all except for meals, or a meeting at his old college. Refilling the nest with a new generation seemed like a very good idea.

Celia, their mother, had a large sunny bedroom downstairs – which was just as well, because she claimed to have the same heart condition that killed her twin, Maud. Celia's bedroom was officially shared with her husband Arthur, but often he could be found camped on his study sofa during the late night or early mornings.

Celia and Maud had been classic identical twins. In adulthood, Celia had become plump, and cut off her long dark braids for a short, wavy hairstyle. Maud kept her lean figure and her long hair, winding thin braids around her head in a halo that was increasingly touched with silver. She wasn't a great age when her heart gave out, quietly, in her sleep – Celia took it as a personal warning to avoid stairs and all kinds of physical exertion. Perhaps it was also the sadness pervading the blue rose-papered little bedroom that now kept her below stairs.

Cassandra gathered the four corners of the dust sheet that held the wallpaper shreds and laboured downstairs with it like a nursery rhyme stork's bundle. She heaved it out the back door, and dragged it down to the back of the garden. The dry, empty husks of last year's acorns crunched under her feet as she trudged to the back hedge, where Robert had raked a large pile of leaves and was watching them smoulder in a small bonfire.

'Add this to your blaze,' Cassandra said.

'Sure,' said Robert, tipping the ash from his lit cigarette onto the ground.

'Give me one of those?'

'Sure, sis, but don't let your mother see.' Robert handed her a fag, and lit it.

They stood side by side and looked at the flames that flared up as the wallpaper caught.

'You kissed me once,' Cassandra said.

'No…'

'Yes, you kissed me at the New Year's dance. You thought I was Athena.'

'I can tell you apart.'

'Beside the obvious current physical difference, how, pray tell?'

'Athena has six freckles on her nose, and you have three. Athena has a scar on her thigh…'

'You haven't seen my thighs.'

'You have slightly thicker and curlier hair than she does, and your voice –'

'What about my voice?'

'Your voice has a brittle tone. Altogether, you are harder and less kind.'

'That why you chose her?'

'I think the gods decided it for us.'

'You can kiss me now.'

Robert raked the blaze with his shovel, covering the embers with ash. 'You just proved my point. That was neither kind nor well-intentioned. I am happily married. To your sister.' He looked up and waved to Athena, who was watching from her bedroom window.

Cassandra threw her cigarette into the fire and stalked back to the house.

In the kitchen, Celia was shelling peas. 'Set the table for lunch, there's a dear,' she said. 'And check how the fowl is doing in the oven.'

Cassandra set about her task, hands full of knives and forks. Her long fingers clutched the bone-handled knives, suddenly white-knuckled with inexplicable rage. *Brittle*, Robert had said.

As brittle as a bird's egg, ready to crack.

'Such a smell of smoke,' complained Celia. 'Will you close the door, love?'

Cassandra had no sooner done that than it opened again, and in walked Jimmy, literally the boy next door. He was an only child, a year younger than Athena and Cassandra, but had been their comrade and third brother through backyard battles and summer camping forays throughout their shared childhood. From his coat pockets he lifted two black and white bundles.

'Kittens?' asked Celia. 'What are you doing with kittens, Jimmy?'

'I rescued them,' Jimmy said, placing the two tiny creatures on

Celia's lap. 'They were going to be drowned. I thought of the kindest lady I know, and brought them straight to you.'

'Ever the silver-tongued rogue,' muttered Cassandra. 'What are we going to do with two kittens?'

'They're very young,' observed Celia. 'Like two peas in a pod. How shall we tell them apart? Are they weaned? Cassandra, pass me that saucer, and the milk jug…a little sugar, top it up with warm water from the kettle…'

The kittens proved themselves capable of slurping milk from a saucer.

'Toxoplasmosis,' said Arthur, walking into the kitchen. 'I wondered what the fuss was about. Cats carry toxoplasmosis.'

'These little scraps aren't old enough to have diseases,' said Celia. 'Look at their dear little paws.' She cradled one of the kittens in her hand. 'Meg,' she said. 'We'll call them Meg and Peg. '

Cassandra scooped up one of the kittens and held it high – looking eye to eye with the little being. A stream of noisome faeces leaked from the animal, staining the bodice of her dress.

'Why must everything in this house come in pairs?' shouted Cassandra. She left the room and bounded upstairs into the maid's room and kicked the door. It bounced on its hinges and stayed ajar. She ripped off the soiled dress and searched her half-packed, half-stored clothes for another.

'Do you think you're…cut out…for nursing?' jeered Jimmy, who had followed.

'I'm not dressed, go away,' Cassandra growled.

'Puuh-lease, I've run naked with you on the lawn.'

'We aren't four years old any more.' Cassandra slammed the door in his face.

When she opened the door, a little calmer, to wash in the bathroom, Athena was there.

'I saw you with Robert in the garden. Don't think you can steal him from me just because I'm fat.'

Cassandra made no reply. In the segmented bathroom mirror, a double image of the sisters, both frowning, reflected mounting anger.

She ran down to the kitchen.

Mother was pouring soup into a china tureen. 'I've strained the broth. Athena's is ready on the tray...'

'Athena doesn't want any lunch.'

'I'll take her some tea...and bread and butter,' said Robert.

'Not yet, she's sleeping,' smirked Cassandra.

'Put a cover on her tray, and take it up later,' Mother instructed.

The meal progressed, soup, then the chicken.

Pudding was crème brûlée, father's favourite. He was cheerful as he cracked the toffee layer and spooned the silky custard. High-pitched mews came from the newspaper-lined shoebox where the kittens had been napping.

'Hungry again,' said Mother. 'Cassandra, better give them a little of the roast chicken meat minced up –'

'No, let Jimmy do it.'

Jimmy, who had stayed for the meal, held the crying kittens as Celia prepared a little dish of meat.

'You're so hard, Cassandra,' said Mother. 'Hard as ice.'

Athena appeared at the door in her dressing gown.

'Why are you out of bed?' Celia left the kittens to Jimmy and began ushering her daughter upstairs.

'Gasping of hunger and thirst!' complained Athena.

'...but you were sleeping...' Robert said.

Cassandra began slowly clearing away as Robert placated Athena with promises of food and an angry look at his sister-in-law's back.

'If looks could kill,' smirked Jimmy.

Cassandra cleared and washed up. Mother had a nap, Father went out for a walk, Jimmy finally went home and Robert was...well, Cassandra didn't know where Robert was, and that wasn't a bad thing. She took her time over the washing up. Standing at the sink beneath the window, she held one of the vegetable dishes, a piece of her mother's wedding china, up to the golden afternoon light and inspected it. Porcelain as thin and fragile as love. She finished washing up and dried the dishes thoroughly, stacking them neatly away.

Jimmy's words had hit home. She knew that nursing wasn't really for her. It had been an impulsive decision…but there must be other paths to freedom. Paths that didn't involve marriage. She had good shorthand and typing, skills that were apparently in demand in the city.

Cassandra looked around the tidy kitchen, then remembered the tray Robert had taken up to Athena.

She went quietly upstairs and found her sister cocooned beneath the green satin eiderdown, dozing. The tray, empty plates smeared with food, teetered on a precarious angle beside her. Cassandra lifted it to the side table, then crept under the eiderdown, spooning her sister's back as they often had as children.

'Robert's gone to church to pray for your soul,' murmured Athena.

'Someone's got to be the bad sister.'

'I hate it when we fight.'

'I just feel…like that time we went boating on the river, and lost an oar…going round in circles…'

'So let go, and float a while.'

'I may jump ship.'

There was a long pause.

Athena took her sister's hand and placed it on her belly. Cassandra could feel the small twitch of tiny limbs beneath the smooth skin.

'Be sure to come back for the miraculous event,' said Athena. 'The new generation will require an audience.'

'Visiting hours only,' said Cassandra. 'We don't want Robert feeling threatened.' She stroked the now still belly, brushed her sister's shoulder with a light kiss and went downstairs, leaving the tray behind.

Her father came in from the garden, hung up his battered hat and asked, 'Any tea?'

Cassandra put the kettle on, and set out two cups and saucers. When they were settled at the table with their steaming beverages, her father was in a rare communicative mood. He placed a warm, dry hand over her moist, reddened one.

'How did you bear it, all this twin-ness?' Cassandra asked softly.

'I love your mother. I love you all.'

'But loving…and bearing…are two different things –'

'Don't wait for a place at the hospital.'

Cassandra suddenly realised, that in all her mother's noisy remonstrations against the boys' enlistment, her father had kept silent. 'You encouraged the boys to leave!'

'Your mother would keep you all safe in the nest, as close as she kept Maud. My dear, if you don't get out of this house, you'll be shadowing your sister for the rest of your life.'

'But how can I…?'

'A quick break is the easiest.' He took a fat envelope from his jacket pocket and slid it across the table. 'I've been saving this for you since you were born. I gave your sister her money on her wedding day.'

'But Athena…'

'Has Robert now. Don't give your mother time to bind you –'

'As she did with you?'

'As she did with Maud. I'm here of my own choice, but poor Maudie…'

'Mother kept Auntie here?'

'With soft bonds of love so strong that nothing could break them. The bonds of twins, as you know… I've been a mere bystander…'

Cassandra stared at her father. He was giving her permission, urging her, to break her mother's heart. To abandon her twin. She watched as he wrote the address of a boarding house on the envelope.

'Live a life of your own, Cass. It'll be worth the pain.'

Cassandra stood and hugged her father. It would be a long time before they were together again. She took the money and tiptoed upstairs, packing swiftly and quietly.

Childhood's secret whistle called Jimmy urgently to her window. He drove her to the railway station and kissed her goodbye on the lips.

Not like a brother at all. His lips were tender and tasted of toffee and tobacco.

'Marry me, Cassie!' Jimmy pleaded.

'Not on your life.'

She was on the train to London with a newspaper, studying the want ads, before Mother woke from her afternoon nap. From the train window, at dusk, Cassandra watched wind-borne autumn leaves scatter onto distant hills. Seabirds rose on strong air currents, ever higher into smoky skies, far towards the coast and the open sea.

Houseboat

Life onboard is slower than that feathered strand of seaweed drifting under the bridge. On the upper deck, I have a comfortable chair in a corner of shade. A book close to hand, sunglasses, hat and a cool drink in progress. A Scrabble board on a low table. All so middle-aged.

There is a rancid smell of rotting fish at this bend of the river. Broken nets are tangled around wet-blackened wharf posts. White, sun-bleached barnacles cover the rock wall above the low tideline. The corrugated wall of the boatshed, heavy with rust, has a definite lean to it where movement in the sandy subsoil has shifted the old Oregon frame from its concrete slab. Rusty crab pots have been left to disintegrate along the river wall, between clumps of drying weed, that will later be collected by local retirees to fertilise their sea-change gardens. Nothing is in a hurry here.

The slow shadow of a dolphin and her baby can be seen gliding beneath the cool green swell. I consider the Scrabble letters standing up to attention in their little wooden pew. Rearrange a few of the ivory tablets.

YAB

BAY

BAB

ABB

BABY – Yes, that'll do fine – BABY. I lay the letters out across the pastel squares on the board, then survey the whole:

FATHER

BREAST

MATERNITY – That had been a coup, building on Brian's four-letter MATE, and capturing a triple word score. I pick my new letters out of the bag. I now have three Ss, and no vowels.

'Your turn,' I call to Brian.

'No, you have it for me, Belinda,' he says, adjusting the rod he holds patiently over the slow-flowing river.

'No way. Get your butt down here,' I reply. 'I'm going down to make coffee.'

I don't fish. And there is a limit to the number of books you can carry on a houseboat. I tried knitting, but the salt air made my hands sticky and the wool refused to glide as it should along my grandma's old blue-steel needles. In desperation, searching through the collection of board games stored under the bench seat in the eating nook, I came up with Scrabble. I begin a game each morning, leisurely played in lieu of the crossword in the morning paper we are usually too far from town to fetch. This ensures occasional comment between us, a thread of staggered conversation at least, during the long, long fishing sessions.

When I return, balancing two melamine mugs of coffee and a packet of gingernuts as I climb to the upper deck, I stare at Brian's new word:

CONCEIVE

Just where is this cruise headed?

When Brian had said he owned a boat, the first image in my mind was of a sailing boat and romantic pink sunsets. Or a sleek, harbour-going catamaran, maybe even a speedboat and waterskis. A widower, he had seemed a safer choice from the dating agency than a thrice-divorced, boutique-beer-drinking IT specialist proudly professing a bizarre sense of humour, and a probable penchant for porn. Not many of the grinning faces peering from the dating website seemed likely long-term companions.

Taking a chance, I met Brian in person, one sunny Sydney morning by the Opera House. We walked to a busy café for coffee and muffins. He seemed reassuringly ordinary, and incredibly proud of the two sons he'd brought up alone.

Straight off, he told me about his vasectomy, in case I was looking to start a family. 'Can't help you there,' he laughed.

I assured him, with a straight, unemotional face, that I was not interested in children. That was water well under the bridge, part of my sad, sorry past. He didn't need to know any of that chapter in my life.

Brian was endearingly excited, but a bit lost, at the prospect of early retirement and a generous redundancy package. When he offered me a holiday on his houseboat, I didn't hesitate. By then, I'd seen the pictures, heard a blow-by-blow account of the refurbishment, and been given an outline of the clever cooking arrangements. This was the most suburban of boats, a floating caravan really, with fitted cupboards, floral cushioned seats around the eating nook and a DVD player where Brian liked to watch reruns of classic westerns in the evening. That was when I did most of my reading. Light romances, historical novels, crime thrillers. I'll read nearly anything that takes me into another life.

Keeping my independence, I had driven through the countryside alone in my car to meet Brian at the boat mooring, reassured to know that I could leave anytime I wanted. But so far I have stayed, a month now, lulled into this slow pace of the endless green river.

Brian is a teetotaller. Allergic to alcohol, actually. This doesn't bother me in the slightest – what a relief on our first dinner date when he paused, embarrassed, over the wine list and then confessed his weakness!

If I never drank another drop in my life, it would be no loss. My husband had liked it…liked it way too much. Lost himself in drink, as the years of our infertility took their toll. And at last slammed his Lexus into a telegraph pole coming home drunk from a business dinner at two a.m. That's the sad story of my life: no husband, no kids, no career – why should I bother with my boring office job any more when Bill's life insurance paid out handsomely and left me a debt-free, property-owning widow at forty-three?

Brian's older than me, a safe choice, but that's OK. We are both free of responsibilities, if not of memories, guilt and a nagging sense of pointlessness. Money is no problem. I own a block of flats in Brisbane that provides a healthy income from rent. I haven't told Brian about that. No need to disclose too much, and he is more than happy to foot the bill for our dates and holidays. We are talking, in a vague way, of an overseas trip next year.

Brian decides to pull in his fishing lines and chug along to the little island mid-river. To be fair, this houseboat can crack along at a decent pace. He has told me all the details of the engine size, but the technicalities rolled over my consciousness like a wave over a pelican's foot. Pulling in close to the muddy shore between the mangroves, we frighten off a flock of gulls. There's a picnic ground in there, according to Brian.

'Come on, let's get our land legs again,' he laughs.

I grin, but seriously, the lack of walking, exercise and all this sitting around on the boat is doing bad things to my waistline. What a blessing Brian isn't a drinker, or sipping wine in the evening would be a real trap.

We drop anchor and clamber between mangroves onto the shore. Small crabs run, startled, for shelter. We find the picnic ground with a covered table and a barbecue. Some firewood has been left, ready for use. I gather some kindling, and we take our time lighting a fire where we cook steaks and onions to eat with tossed salad and bread. Seagulls hover, of course, wanting to share our food. It is a pleasant meal, despite the constant flies. I try to identify the many bird sounds, but apart from a kookaburra, I can't name any. After a while, we hear human voices above the squawking gulls. The voices become louder, and eventually two figures emerge from the tea tree scrub. A young woman in a tie-dyed sarong and bikini carrying a baby in a Moses basket, followed by a bare-chested, esky-carrying man in fluoro board shorts. They greet us like old friends.

'So bloody glad to see ya!' the man exclaims as he slouches onto our picnic bench, uninvited.

'We've walked and walked for miles,' the woman continues. 'The ferry left without us.'

The story unfolds as they finish off the remnants of our food. They had gone on a day cruise, but somehow the ferry had forgotten them.

'Barry and I had a nap,' says the darkly tanned woman, with a wink. 'That's his name, Barry, and I'm Bernice. And you are? Really? Cute, isn't it? All Bs! Anyways…we had a nap in the shade after I fed the baby at morning tea. When we woke up, everyone was gone.'

Barry opens his esky and pulls out a bottle of beer. He offers one to me, but I shake my head. To my amazement, Brian accepts one and takes three large, swift gulps. He won't meet my eye.

'You will help us get back to town, won't you?' asks Bernice, sidling up to Brian.

We hadn't planned to go back to the fishing village for at least three days, but what choice have we? During the long hot afternoon, we chug against the tide back to the little township. The baby cries, sucking relentlessly on a pacifier, and can't seem to settle. We take her below (it is a girl, dressed in hideous lolly-pink nylon) and sponge her tiny sticky body with tepid water until she is less fractious. Bernice makes up a bottle from supplies in their esky and I offer to feed the infant. At last the baby is calm and sleeps in the basket as I watch her tiny fingers open and close like little crab claws testing the air.

Back in town, our passengers are in no hurry to separate. Barry jogs to the ferry car park and returns with their car, but then as a thank you insists on shouting us all to fish and chips for dinner. He and Brian drive off together to collect the food. Bernice and I make another baby bottle and again I give it to the child.

'Molly, her name is Molly,' says Bernice adjusting her sarong, '…although I keep thinking another B name might be cute instead to match us, Bernice, Barry and… maybe Bindy?'

'How old is she?' I ask.

'Around two months…you'd think I'd have the name settled by now, wouldn't you? But it's not easy, you know. The kid's gonna be saddled with the name her whole life. We're having a babymoon, you know… some time out. I have to decide soon, and do the paperwork, but, or we don't get the childcare benefits. Should have done it already. But I will. Do you like the name Bindy?'

'Sure,' I say.

'I'm glad to have a girl,' Bernice continued. 'Easier than a boy.'

'She's…not your first then?' I ask.

'Na, I've a boy, Brendan. He's a real handful, naughty little bugger…lives with his grandma…his dad's mum she is, not mine. Barry don't wanna raise another man's child…'

The men are away a long time. I hear Bernice's life story. My resentment builds as she finishes the last of the beer. I drink iced water. Bernice seems to be as fertile as a fish – and the children, if they are allowed to arrive in this world, are a bother to her rather than a blessing. I reflect on all those years my late husband and I tried, month after month, to conceive. Never being blessed. Never having what other people so effortlessly achieve.

When the men do come back, complaining of long queues at the fish and chip shop, it is obvious that they have also been at the local pub. They are roaring and laughing like old mates. It is all way too familiar for comfort. Allergic to alcohol! Lapsed AA member, more like. We eat the greasy food inside, but the night is muggy and the houseboat stifling. Bernice is drinking glass after glass of cheap cask wine.

I take the baby up into the cooler air on deck as the sun sets, and rock her in my arms. There's a gentle breeze over the still river. When she sleeps, she rests on my shoulder until I go into the bedroom to change her nappy. She sleeps peacefully on the bed. Quietly and calmly I gather my clothes and valuables. There isn't much. I line my large canvas beach bag with a pillow. In the kitchen, there is a game of poker beginning and more beer being swilled. From the roars of laughter and the shouts, I learn that they are playing strip poker. Through the porthole, I observe that Bernice is without her sarong already.

I tuck the sleeping infant into my beach bag – she doesn't stir. I walk softly out onto the deck and nudge the empty Moses basket with my foot. All it takes is one tip for the basket, bottle, soft toy and all to roll, silently and predictably, across the few centimetres of deck, under the too-high safety bar and plop into the silent river. I pluck the oversized dummy from the baby's slack lips and toss it in. It floats, pink ribbon trailing like a weird jelly-fish tentacle. A nice touch of pathos, I think.

Inside, the drinkers roar and hoot – Bernice is pulling at the first string on her bikini top. It will be ages before she even thinks about the child.

The gravel slides beneath my feet as I crunch stealthily to my car. I place my bags and the sleeping baby carefully on the back seat. As a truck rumbles past, I turn the ignition key and without headlights, roll out onto the road.

Once out of the township, I turn on the headlights, glance at the sleeping child and say thank you to the full, gleaming moon. There is no other traffic. I drive swiftly inland, to the first large town with an all-night chemist. I have plenty of cash in my wallet. It is easy to buy hair dye, formula, nappies, and another pacifier and even a fresh cotton suit for the child.

At a half-empty roadhouse, I use the parent's room to change and feed the baby. Her eyes are brown, like mine. She looks concentratedly at my face as she sucks the bottle dry. I sense that a deal is being made between us. Already she recognises me as a reliable source of food. I rub instant hair colour into my short bob. I was never a natural blonde. I change into a plain white shirt and dark trousers, creating quite a different look to the bright summer gear I wore on the houseboat. For good measure, I remove my contact lenses and put on my dark-rimmed glasses. In the small grimy mirror, I see a reliable, middle-aged face.

My phone beeps with a message, but without even looking at the caller's name, I take out the sim card and flush it. I smash the phone against the tiled wall and wrap the shattered remains into the soiled nappy, and post the smelly bundle into the bin provided. As I wash my hands with sharp-scented lemon soap, I feel free, cleansed, energised. More alive than I have been for a long, long time. I am finally a winner in the game of life.

Back in the car, we head north. We will be home at my Brisbane apartment before long. I want to get as many miles behind us as possible in the dark. No one will find us. They won't know where to look for me – and all evidence points to a small drowned body in the river. To be safe, I will ditch this car and drive my poor dead husband's second car, a Mercedes, still stored in the apartment basement. Why I kept it, I couldn't have told you – but useful now. I can register the birth and make up a story about a fertility clinic, using stored sperm, and hospital records getting mislaid. The people who know me well will believe my story – they know how hard I tried for a child all those years. I've been away from Queensland and out of touch for two years, so it will all sound plausible. No need to change my name. I'd never told Brian my real name anyway, and he never knew I came from Brisbane. I had talked a lot about Melbourne, where I worked for a while, as if it were my hometown. He knows me only by the alias I made up for the dating agency. With the pounding head he will have tomorrow, he may not even remember that.

There is plenty of time to dream and plan as we travel along the night roads through sleepy towns with all the windows darkened and front doors locked. I consider our future, the playdates, the schools, the life we will share. The story I will tell about her conception. There will be no need to ever confess or contact a biological mother, if my baby doesn't know about the river, the houseboat, and the birth mother who couldn't even decide on a name for her daughter.

My daughter.

Mentally, I review all the names I had considered when planning for a child. None of them seem appropriate for this dark-eyed angel. Something will occur to me, I am sure. I play with letters and initials that will go with my surname. No rush to decide. Something classic and serene and unobjectionable.

The baby makes a little noise in her sleep, but doesn't wake. One thing is for sure, neither my baby, nor I, will ever again answer to a name beginning with the letter B.

Movement

Marguerite was at the gynaecologist's when the earthquake struck. The nurse was asking about her children, their ages, progress and activities; Marguerite was perched on the end of the examination table; the speculum had just been inserted and the doctor about to take the pap smear. A second later, the table capsized and Marguerite was thrust sideways onto the cold floor. Her cotton robe slid across the polished vinyl surface, leaving her wedged against the doctor's desk.

The nurse was silent; it was obvious from her misshapen skull and the angle of her broken neck that Sister Ann would never cheer a nervous patient with happy conversation again. She had taken the full force of the heavy beam supporting the roof, which now lay across the surgery, forming an oblique triangle of the once spacious, light-filled room. Dr Kosiak crawled under the fallen beam and felt Sister Ann's twisted neck for a pulse. Finding none, he snapped off the harsh examination light that had still been burning, spotlighting the nurse's poor, pale, surprised face.

In the black, airless space, there was silence. At last, Marguerite heard him crawl towards her and crouch beside the desk.

Are you all right, Marguerite?

Yes. Nothing broken. But I still have this lump of metal in me.

Dr Kosiak grunted. He crawled back to the light. Marguerite heard the switch being flicked, but no light came.

The doctor was at her side again. *Never mind, I can do this with my eyes closed.*

She knew he wasn't lying – this doctor had looked after her since she first visited these rooms twenty years ago, a naive young woman, miscarrying her first pregnancy. He had been the one who couldn't find a heartbeat for that first, unfinished foetus. He had monitored each successive pregnancy and checked the movement of each baby in her womb. He had delivered her sons, a lead player in these significant highs and lows of her life.

She felt his chunky fingers pat along the floor and find her left leg. *Just lift up a bit.*

It was awkward, crammed as they were against the faux-timber desk, but in a moment the implement was removed and Marguerite sighed with relief. For once, no awkward moment of eye contact, no wondering where to look. There is no protocol for this, Marguerite considered. Where does one look when a doctor, a dentist, or podiatrist is doing personal things to one's body? Perhaps these procedures should always take place in the dark.

A moment later the shivering set in.

Are you cold?

No.

You're in shock.

Dr Kosiak crawled under the beam and groped for his coat, which had been hanging on a rack behind the door. He dragged it back and covered Marguerite with it. Her fingers, shaking, grabbed the coarse tweed and pulled it tight around her body.

Now that the light had been extinguished, they could see three pinpricks of light where the window had been.

How long before we're rescued?

It will be a while, I should think. At least we have air.

They sat in silence. Marguerite was still shaking and becoming cold now, but tried to focus on the three points of light forming a little triangle high up to her right.

Marguerite heard him scrabbling around in the dark, the screech of something being dragged over a hard surface. A little crash to the left of her made her jump.

Sorry. The phone's dead.

Doctor Kosiak crawled back to Marguerite and sat beside her. *You're still shivering.* He put his arm around her shoulders for warmth. *Don't worry. We'll just sit tight till someone comes.*

There was a strong smell like burnt rubber but Marguerite tried to ignore the possibility of fire. As her eyes became more and more accustomed to the dark, she could see the crumpled shape of Sister Ann like an abandoned marionette in the corner of the room. *Mustn't cry,* she told herself. Think of something else. Like looking at the pictures of green ferny waterfalls on the ceiling whilst in the dentist's chair. She flexed her legs and clenched her naked buttocks, cold on bare floor. How odd to be sitting like this, undressed, in the dark beside a man not her husband. She rested against the warmth of him. Marguerite could hear the steady intake of his breath, feel the movement of his chest with every exhale. Some women fantasised about their gynaecologists, but she had always thought of Dr Kosiak more as a father figure than a lover. Not that he was that much older than she. The spicy scent of his aftershave seemed to grow stronger in her nostrils. Even now, almost naked beside him… no, it was no use looking for her clothes. They had been left on a chair near the blocked doorway, where Sister Ann lay. Wonder what had happened at home? Where were Brian and the boys? Must call…

Peter (she knew Dr Kosiak's first name but had never called him by it in twenty years), *Peter, is my handbag on the floor? Can you find it? My mobile is in it…perhaps we can…?*

Dr Kosiak crawled around in the awkward spaces between fallen rubble and furniture, cursing as a sharp object tore at his trousers and he cracked his head on an open filing cabinet drawer. *This it?* he asked, pushing a soft leather form into her hands.

This was something she could do with her eyes closed. The phone was in the side pocket, as always. She pressed the buttons and heard the dial tone. It was then the tears began to flow.

Marguerite's family were fine; their house only slightly damaged. She phoned emergency services.

Do you want to phone your wife? She knew, from past conversations, he was married.

No need, she didn't survive. As a siren sounded outside the building, Dr Peter Kosiak stared at the crumpled form of Sister Ann, bowed his head, and wept.

Dinner Plates for One Hundred and Thirty

'What about these?' Anne emerged from the pantry, carrying a dusty box. It held six black, white and gold plates, all different, all decorated with musical motifs. One looked like a vinyl record, one swirled with staves, notes and clefs, another had song lyrics – Anne didn't even bother looking at the rest.

'Yes, anything you can find,' said Linda. 'We need every plate in the house.'

There was a party on. Linda's partner Pete's seventieth birthday. Family was coming from far-flung places, old friends from interstate, neighbours from up and down the street.

'How many people?' asked Anne.

'I've given up trying to count,' Linda said. 'Your father keeps inviting more… People are so unreliable these days, they say yes but mean no, they forget, or invite their partner and bring their kids… It could be thirty or one hundred and thirty.'

'We should've got caterers and hired everything,' said Anne.

'He didn't want a fuss! Just family, he said, but then it snowballed…'

'Disposable plates would be a lot simpler,' said John, walking in with a box of odd dinner plates. Still single, John was the youngest of the family, the son of Linda and Pete. The baby. He put his box of plates on the kitchen bench with a thump. 'Some of them are chipped,' he said.

'They'll do,' said Anne. 'We're desperate.' She pointed to the dining room table stacked with piles: the 'best' Wedgwood floral china plates, everyday white ones, brown pottery platters not used since the seventies, Christmas ones decorated with holly and poinsettias, bright solid-colour fiesta ware, and a pile of mismatched op-shop blue and white willow pattern from a decorating fad of Anne's a few years back. At the bottom of the 'everyday' pile there was a melamine Thomas the Tank Engine plate and another that memorialised John's kindergarten effort at a self-portrait. As Linda said, they were desperate. Anne lifted each plate from John's box, inspected it and polished off any dust and grime with a tea towel, before adding it to a pile.

'Disposable plates would be easier,' repeated John.

'Your father will not abide plastic plates,' Linda said. 'You know he's a mad keen conservationist now. He's at war with single-use plastics. He inspects the rubbish bin for recycling mistakes. It would spoil the party for him.'

'Paper?' suggested Anne.

'They go soggy and break,' said Linda. 'Especially as Janelle is bringing wet dishes.'

'I've seen ones made from bamboo,' John said.

'But where do you buy them?' asked Linda. 'Oh, what about the picnic basket? I think it's in the garage.'

'Yes!' Anne scurried to the garage on a mission.

John picked up a fork from a basket on the table, and twirled it like a baton. 'Good thing Dad was scavenging cutlery at garage sales for his garden sculptures.'

'They came up sparkling from the dishwasher,' Linda agreed. She laughed, and then plonked herself into a chair.

"Worn out already?" John asked his mother.

"Yes, but Anne is a big help.'

'Janelle?'

'She's bringing food,' Linda replied. She and Janelle, the eldest step-daughter, had a less harmonious relationship.

'Want me to phone her for plates?' John was a favourite with them all.

'Please!' said Linda. 'I've still got to hunt out enough glasses.'

'Okay,' said John pulling out his phone. 'Plates *and* glasses. Then I'll deal with the fairy lights.'

At six p.m, Janelle arrived carrying two crockpots steaming with curry, a large bag of uncooked rice, six melamine wine glasses and an economy pack of a hundred plastic plates.

'One vegetarian curry, one normal,' she explained.

'Don't say normal,' said John. 'That's a value judgement.'

'Whatever! I need a pot to cook the rice.'

In one swift movement, Linda hid the plastic plates in the pot drawer and lifted out a large saucepan. She handed it to Janelle with a smile. 'I'm going up to shower and change,' she said. 'Your grandmother is already in the lounge. Keep an eye on her? I'll be quick.'

Linda jogged upstairs, pushed the bedroom door closed with her behind, and kicked off her shoes. The grimy clothes she had been working in since six a.m. came off and lay discarded where they fell. The hot shower was soothing. At sixty-one, she was slim apart from her droopy pot belly, healthy except for aches and pains when tired. She was tired now. How tempting to linger under the steaming water! But guests were arriving, Pete's mother already installed downstairs. Linda rinsed shampoo from her hair and turned off the water. She towelled her skin dry. There was nothing she wanted more than just to slip into bed and doze. But it couldn't be done…she had responsibilities.

She rubbed her short blonde-grey hair vigorously and ran her fingers through it, hoping to create some volume. Pete's brothers and their partners were invited, and she hadn't seen them for years. They had all aged, but…somehow Linda always felt dowdy in their company. She shook off these thoughts and brushed her teeth, smoothed on makeup with practised speed, applied mousse and blow-dried her hair in record time. She put on the outfit that was waiting on the bed: slim black trousers and a black tunic with trumpet sleeves, embroidered at the edges with glistening jet-like beads. Looking at her image in the mirror, she wound a long silk scarf, in shades of peacock blue and jade, around her neck. A little warmth and colour wouldn't go astray.

Linda looked at her bare hands. She didn't routinely wear rings, although she had a selection of sterling silver sculptural pieces and a large solitaire sapphire Pete had given her. No wedding band. They'd never married, although living together for decades.

'You might want out,' Pete had said, in the early days when he was alone with the girls, and they had been a handful, Janelle especially. 'You might want to throw in the towel,' Pete had warned. 'Divorce is messy, why put up fences we don't need?'

So they lived as a family without the ceremony, and she had stayed, and they had fallen into the routines and habits and patterns of suburban existence, with their little foibles and resentments and loves. When John was born, he was given his father's surname, and Linda gradually, unofficially, added it with a hyphen to her own, to smooth school communications and so on, but she never officially changed it. Pete insisted that the house they bought together be legally hers, as recognition of her investment in their shared life. It could not be taken from her.

Linda left her silver rings in the drawer. There would be so much kitchen work: washing, drying hands, mopping up spills. Better to have bare hands that slid easily in and out of the rubber gloves.

Ninety-two-year-old Muriel was indeed in the lounge room, alone. After kisses and embraces, she had been led to a recliner in the lounge and given a cup of tea and a shortbread. Her son sat in the matching recliner, also sipping tea, and together they watched tennis on the TV.

Anne's children arrived: three-year-old Marcus and the baby Isabelle. A placid baby, Isabelle was content to sit on her great grandmother's lap and play peekaboo.

Marcus, a little wary, walked around and around, lent over to Muriel and whispered in her ear, 'You're very old.'

'Yes, indeed I am,' replied Muriel, chuckling, wondering at the absurdity of it: that her little chap who had looked so much like Marcus was now seventy years young.

Muriel had something important to say. She kept repeating it in her mind so that it wouldn't drift away, just as she had put the unlooked-for letter in her handbag beside Pete's birthday card. The letter with foreign stamps, that had arrived in her mailbox. The letter from her lost daughter-in-law. The letter that Muriel had answered, in careful copperplate and well-chosen words, giving Pete's address.

But these little ones were on her lap, circling her chair – distracting! Oh, how sweetly! With hot little lips pressed on her wrinkled cheek and little fingers brushing her bare forearm for attention. Not shy. Oh no, not in the least, although they met her so rarely. Muriel had something important to tell her son, Pete, but he was preoccupied with grandchildren and their hand-drawn birthday wishes, and then he was out on an errand and the opportunity was lost.

The two little ones were taken off to be babysat by their father's parents. They were too young to stay up so late. Their parents would have a child-free night.

Humph, thought Muriel. *In our day there was no such thing. Parenting was a constant. Not like these days, not like…what was that one's name again? The one who –*

Muriel, her tea drunk and half a shortbread nibbled, the rest of it a soggy sludge in the bottom of her teacup where it had fallen when she dunked it, rested back in her chair. She pushed the button that moved the chair to a lying position. She dozed.

Muriel opened her eyes. She wanted to confront her son about the lie he had maintained for thirty years…maybe more? Dates seem to swim in a sea of turbulent waves these days. The lie he told his children. *I will find him later*, she thought. *But it must be tonight.* Time suddenly seemed short, and the need for truth imperative. Exhausted by the children, Muriel closed her eyes again. Hold the thought. Pete would return and she would tell him *the important thing*.

Pete had told his daughters the story of their mother's accidental death so often that he almost believed it himself. A freak wave had washed Ava far out to sea from a remote beach in Thailand and she was lost forever. No body, no grave.

Her family believed it, the children believed it, his siblings, too… only his mother made him confess privately to the lie. Ava had simply abandoned them. She didn't want to return to Australia and her suburban life, motherhood and domestic doldrums. She took a few things in a batik tote bag and walked away.

In his grief, Pete had constructed a story that was outlandish but believable because of his real, stunned mourning. He and the children had been the recipients of kind support and sympathy from family and neighbours, and a steady stream of single women clucking over his girls.

Muriel dozed.

Linda had sent Pete out for ice.

He rejected the notion of buying sparkling wine for a toast. 'No speeches,' he had said. 'It isn't that sort of party.'

His children wanted all the bells and whistles. He wanted just a gathering of friends to share his good fortune of being alive and healthy. So many were less lucky. They arrived in his head at odd times, the memories of dead mates and past lovers. There had been many women before he settled down with Linda. Some faces had no names as they stared at him in the slideshow that passed under his closed eyelids in the twilight this side of sleep. Linda was a blessing, one that felt undeserved. He gave in and drove to the bottle shop to buy bubbly. Let the kids have their celebration, what did it matter?

Pete had borrowed folding tables and chairs from neighbours up and down the street. Since retiring, he'd volunteered in the community garden, bush care, neighbourhood watch and every other local group. He knew everyone and had invited them all. Fairy lights were strung on lintels and posts, around the branches of the lemon tree, the eucalypts and the banksias. Solar garden lights illuminated the pathways and garden beds. It looked magical.

Linda had reserved the table on the veranda with the most comfortable chairs in a sheltered spot for her mother-in-law and immediate family. She went in search of Muriel. The old woman was still lying in the recliner.

'I'm stuck like a turtle on my back,' the old woman complained. 'I can't find the button to get this thing upright again!'

There were so many people at the party: acquaintances, faces Linda half remembered, had never met or who were so changed by age that she had no idea who they were. The woman with long dyed-red locks and silver bracelets who went to sit on the veranda beside Muriel was a complete mystery. There was something familiar about her face…but no information was forthcoming from a dredge of Linda's usually reliable memory. She must find Pete and ask him who that woman was.

Ava flicked her long red hair over one shoulder and rested back in her chair. She leant over and arranged a cushion behind her mother-in-law's back. The old lady thanked her then peered closely into her face and whispered: 'Oh, it's *you*.'

No one else had recognised her. Ava had bought a bottle of whisky so as not to arrive empty-handed, but on the bus, she had opened it and topped up her takeaway coffee. Ava had chosen the seat beside Muriel partly for camouflage, partly due to the dim light offered from one large candle in a glass hurricane lantern. She had been greeted by a young man and handed a glass of wine. Too easy, fortified by whisky and longing, to walk in and take her place at the table beside the old woman. What would happen next was anyone's guess. Muriel could spill the beans and save her the trouble of introductions. The girls – women now – were busy and hadn't noticed her. Why would they? As far as they knew, she was a weed-decorated skeleton at the bottom of the ocean.

Ava could hear Pete's unmistakable laugh echo up the yard from where he stood with a group of men beneath the fairy-lit trees. Some things never changed. She swallowed the last of her wine.

The slim woman in black, Pete's new partner, so Ava assumed, came to the table and invited them to the buffet.

'I'll get you a plate, Muriel,' Ada offered. She stood and slipped away as Linda and Muriel greeted two couples to the table. Ava wasn't sure, they could be relatives. It was all so long ago.

Janelle was ladling curry and rice onto plates. Ada accepted two, without making eye contact. How like Ada's own mother Janelle looked! And the identical mannerisms with which she spooned the food! Even though that grandmother had died before Janelle was born. Nature over nurture. Ada stumbled back to the veranda table, plates brimming with hot food and face warm with unexpected emotion.

Muriel sampled her curry and made appreciative noises. Ada began to eat, but couldn't taste anything. Her throat was swollen and tight. She forked rice into her mouth and chewed, emptying her plate robotically. In the candlelight, she began to see glimmers on the plate beneath the curry. Gold and black…a swirling pattern…a treble clef… She ate faster. She took a paper napkin and wiped away the last smear of sauce. She stared, stunned, at the plate.

Fifty years ago, Ada had given Pete a commemorative set of twenty-four-carat plates celebrating his favourite song. They had cost a bomb. They were collector's pieces meant for a display cabinet, not an outdoor party. She had just eaten Janelle's curry and rice from one of them.

The plate and the table seemed to spin. She stood, and the fairy-lit yard was a blur of light and sound. Muriel, still slowly working her way through her meal, didn't notice as her daughter-in-law slipped away, down the back steps, through the crowd and out the side gate.

Down in the garden, Anne looked up and saw a shadowy figure, resembling the ghost who haunted her dreams. The shadow figure retreated into darkness.

'All right, love?' asked her father.

Yes, of course,' replied Anne. 'Happy birthday, Dad!'

Pete kissed his daughter, then wandered up and sat in the empty chair beside Muriel. He looked down at the dinner plate in front of her, smeared with the remains of curry. It was unfamiliar and yet known to him, all at the same time.

Muriel leant over. 'There's something important I need to say to you,' she said. 'About that first one.'

Pete wondered whether the old dear was quite with it. 'Yes, Mum, what is it?'

Muriel burped. She looked tired. 'I'll remember in a minute,' she said. 'It's in my handbag, with your card.'

She's giving me extra birthday money, Pete decided. *That's all it is.*

Janelle came out with a platter of sausage rolls. They should have been on the buffet, but Linda had been slow getting them out of the oven. 'Who was that, Dad?' she asked. 'The redhead with the bracelets?'

'No idea,' said Pete. 'Probably came with one of the bush care blokes.'

'She's gone,' mumbled Muriel. 'Too late. Ava's gone.'

Pete looked into his mother's cloudy eyes. The candle flame in the lantern flickered.

Linda appeared, carrying a slab cake lit with a forest of candles.

Outside in the street, Ada heard their off-key singing of 'Happy Birthday'. She took a last look at the house that was not hers, every window bright with lights, then turned away. If she walked to the end of the street and turned left onto the main road, she had a chance of hailing a taxi or finding a bus. As she stumbled in the gloom, the wiped-clean gold and black dinner plate, swirling with unsung quavers and clefs, clanked in her tote bag against a half-empty bottle of whisky.

Little Lives

'Basic black for the first day of term?'

'Yep.' I gave Helena a cursory nod and spooned the instant coffee.

Better not to comment on the flowery tent she was wearing this morning. I sniffed the milk from the office fridge, and poured in a generous dash. Helena did try, I know, having dresses made by a professional dressmaker, instead of the polyester sacks many women of her bulk settled for. Being twenty-five, single and a size eight somehow made me an open target for comment, and I resented it. Yes, count my blessings, young and healthy. Be kind to the middle-aged spinster doing the best she can.

Hands around the hot mug, I cradled my resentment in a spot of sunlight warming the grey-green kitchenette lino. Helena prepared her Earl Grey, black, with a thin slice of fresh lemon in a fine china mug.

'Black today? Who died?' Janet walked in with her violin case under her arm.

She's strings; I'm woodwind. Helena is vocal coach, piano tutor, conductress, senior music mistress. With a flourish of a silk batik sleeve, Janet placed a new jar of her fake coffee on the bench. My own new jar of Nescafé stood brightly virtuous on the sink. Really, I thought, the fuss she makes. I only steal a spoon of her muck in an emergency.

'Yes, black. My optimism died about six forty-five this morning when the alarm went off.' Honestly! Can't a girl put on a pencil skirt, a pair of classic high-heeled black leather pumps, and a black blazer on a weekday morning without comment? Thank goodness I took the extra minutes to wash my hair under the shower this morning, or they'd be onto my grooming next. I flicked a long shining strand over my shoulder.

'Meeting in five,' called Janet on her way into the front office. 'See you in the staffroom.'

'Don't suppose we could miss it?'

Helena shook her grey wispy head. 'We'd be missed. Once more into the breach, dear friends…'

I gulped my coffee and fetched a notepad and pen for doodling, wishing for colleagues born AFTER the change to decimal currency, who knew no Latin quotations and absolutely no lines of Shakespeare AT ALL.

I sat next to the new science teacher, Trent, the only other person on staff remotely in the vicinity of thirty years old. What a relief to find a new young face this term! A boarder at this ladies' college for two years while my parents worked overseas, I studied music then came back as a teacher. Such a small circumference to my life: I'm ashamed as I answer Trent's attentive questions. He invited me to lunch. I knew that the girls would make me pay, on the evidence of my uneaten glad-wrapped peanut butter sandwich in the fridge, but my black heels needed an outing so I climbed into his sports car and zoomed down the road for a pub lunch. It was a pupil-free day, so there were no students to notice us as we snuck back onto the school campus and into the science labs, locking the door and pulling down the blind.

A glass case of leaves stood beneath the window. I peered through the gleaming walls.

'One of my phasmids,' said Trent. 'Lucinda. There she is… I've more at home.'

He took the stick insect out of the case and placed her on my arm. Lighter than air, like a little creeping twig she ducked and trembled.

'Do you walk them on a leash?'

'No.' He returned the insect to her glass cell. He checked the thermometer in the tank. 'A bit cold for her,' he said, turning on a heat lamp. 'See the eggs?' He pointed to the small, shiny black ovals on the leaves. 'I wrote my thesis on parthenogenesis.'

I raised my eyebrows in query.

'The female can reproduce without mating,' he explained.

'Sounds like a boring existence,' I laugh.

'Brandy?'

I sat on the bench as Trent poured the thick liquid into two green coffee mugs. 'Camouflage,' he said, handing them both to me.

I sat, both hands full, as he kissed me deeply and sighed. He ran his hands over my skull gathering my long straight hair between his fingers, winding it into a thick rope. Kissing me again, his skilled hands were inside my clothes, inside my bra before I knew what was happening. Not that I minded. This was different to the Friday night fumblings in front of the televised football match I had with Evan, his climaxes timed to fall in the ad breaks. Evan didn't know or care about the function of a clitoris.

Trent knew. He stroked me to the brink of orgasm. He even apologised for the way my head buffeted against the stainless-steel surface of the bench as he then rode to his own rhythm. I never made it back to work that afternoon. We finished the brandy and left, eating ravioli in a bistro in Little Collins Street then spending the night at Trent's brand-new, unfurnished apartment on the river. When I woke in sunlight on the mattress laid in the middle of the gleaming timber floor, I knew life had changed.

Trent did have more insects. A whole menagerie of them. In the bare apartment, they were the only permanent-looking fixture, besides a wall of textbooks and a computer in his study. A mountain bike rested against the wall.

He showed me a stack of over-sized anatomical drawings in chrome frames that he had drawn to illustrate his thesis. Cross-section of an aphid, parts of a stick insect, wing patterns of a moth, anatomy of a ladybird...

'Do you draw people?' I laughed and dropped the towel I was wrapped in.

'I can always learn,' Trent replied, dragging me to the mattress.

*

Breakfast. I wish I had eaten some. There's a yawning hole in my stomach and the coffee is just swooshing around in it like a washing machine on a low water load. Not that there was anything really to eat at home – none of my flatmates have done any shopping for weeks. We are all 'seeing someone' and eating out, or else not eating to keep thin. A bit of toast maybe…

I rummage in the office fridge – Janet's salads and soy yoghurts for the week…she'd notice if I took one of those. At the back, my neglected peanut butter sandwich from last week. It will have to do.

I stood at the window and chewed the dry bread, removing fragments of nut from my left molar with my tongue.

It's quiet in the music department, I'm first to arrive. Couldn't sleep, after giving Evan the shove. He took it badly, and stormed out without even checking the football draw. I tossed and turned all night. I cleansed my conscience in a hot shower, then walked alone through the waking city. Watched the pigeons scrummage for crumbs on the cracked footpath, envied the early morning camaraderie amongst the stall holders at Queen Victoria Markets. At the tram stop, I watched bakers delivering fragrant croissants and news-sellers collecting change from commuters in exchange for the papers they use as a privacy screen and then leave folded, wedged in the crack of the vinyl seat. As my tram pulled away, I saw the lonely head of a camel being unloaded to give rides to children and tourists visiting the markets. How do camels fare in the winter? Can they store heat in their fatty humps as well as moisture?

I thought of Mum and Dad in their island dream world, working in Samoa, living simply and loving it and each other so desperately. I remembered my long-ago schooldays under thatched roofs with no walls; walks on white beaches with dark-skinned children, frangipani blossoms and fishing with Dad on the brimming tide. Boarding school had increased the distance between us beyond mere kilometres. So long I've been in this grey city alone.

Like a dromedary wishing for the desert, I hovered around the heater as it began to provide warmth. I removed my coat, rinsed my mug and let the hot water run over my fingers. As I dried my hands on the small towel Janet launders freshly every week, I heard the footsteps of the two women coming down the corridor. I took a clarinet from the storeroom, adjusted the reed and began limbering up.

'You're bright and early this morning! Trying out the new ensemble arrangement?' Janet asked.

I nodded.

'Are you all right?' asked Helena.

'A bit green around the gills?' wondered Janet.

'A little tired, maybe,' I acknowledged.

'How's Evan?'

I might as well tell them, get it over, I thought. 'I dumped him.'

'Oh?'

'Well, we never thought he was really right for you, did we, Janet? Someone a little bit…intellectual is more your style.'

'That Trent, the new science teacher…there's one for you…'

'Well… yes. Trent has asked me out.'

'Ah! I knew it!' Helena exclaimed, winking at Janet. 'There'll be wedding cake in the common room yet…a spring wedding…just perfect…'

'I'll start knitting the bootees…'

I'm gone from the room with the clarinet before this nonsense can annoy me any further. Meddling witches! Why can't they leave me alone?

*

We escorted year twelve to a concert in the city. Afterwards, having dismissed the girls to their buses, we escaped to a café warmed by a wood-burning stove. The thin arcs of the chair legs stood like frightened colts ready to bolt under Helena's bulk. We ordered sweet ricotta cannoli, panforte, Janet's soy decaf, Helena's black Earl Grey. The waitress apologised for having no fresh lemon. I ordered tea as well.

'Not coffee today?' inquired Janet.

'No, it doesn't sit well on my stomach just now.'

'Oh… I do hope you aren't coming down with something? It's been a terrible winter for flu.'

'No, it isn't flu.' And all in a rush I told them, as I had told Mum and Dad in a late-night phone call to Samoa the night before. That I had done the most foolish cliché of a thing and slept with Trent au naturelle – no pill, no condom, just him, me and the science lab. Well, I didn't tell any of them about the science lab, but I told them I was pregnant and that we were keeping the child. Being truly conservative and getting married to preserve our jobs at the ladies' college before anyone suspected. Maybe I realised that I needed these gossips on my side, or maybe I had underestimated them but they were brilliant: sympathetic but practical, supportive and discreet. We left the café to tour the shops and choose my wedding dress. My self-absorbed flatmates took on the role of bridesmaids but my music teacher colleagues worked tirelessly to arrange a wedding in four weeks flat. My parents flew in from Samoa the day before the ceremony.

'Sorry we can't stay longer, darling,' Mum sighed. She adjusted my veil. 'Are you going to be all right? This is all so *sudden*. You *are* sure, aren't you? It is not too late, even now…you can always catch the flight back to Samoa with us tonight…'

'Yes, Mum, it's fine. I'm happy. How could I not be?'

'Well, if you are sure… Goodness, here's Dad all glammed up… you do look lovely, both of you…goodness, how am I going to survive in these *heels*?'

Marriage is like a paper cup full of fizzy drink – lemonade – no, that's too insipid. The metallic aftertaste of Diet Coke? Feel the sodium benzoate tainting your body, hear the fizzes, the bubbles bursting against the roof of your mouth, your caffeine headache abating. Feel virtuous, no calories added to your daily intake, except the Pringles and smoked salmon dip that you ate because, after all, this is a celebration of marriage.

Roll the home video of the wedding day, bride's veil horizontal in the wind, the groom perspiring with nerves in his satin-lapelled suit, bridesmaids' make-up smudging and the bride's mother aching for a seat to rest her poor blistered feet. She can barely hobble around the dance floor. Toss confetti over everyone. Overdressed children pick up fallen handfuls of the stuff mixed with gravel from the circular drive. Throw the bouquet of orchids to Helena, time for the final wave.

We spent four days in Sorrento for our honeymoon. By then, morning sickness was really taking hold. Trent jogged along the windswept coast and I read and watched the world from behind double-glazed hotel windows. Each night, Trent ran a slow hand over my abdomen, then slept as I lay awake listening to the sea.

On one of my frequent trips to the bathroom, I noticed a brown splodge on the white sink as I spewed love messages to the Genuine Vitreous China. I peered closer, wiping the bile from my lips. It was a brown moth, tiny wings flattened and squashed against the chrome faucet, made slimy with water spray.

The next week, we were both back at school, distributing wedding cake. Helena and Janet cooed over the photos. They gave me their present.

'Didn't want to give it to you on the day,' they said. 'Wanted to explain…'

'It's a samovar,' they said in unison, as I unwrapped a tall brass urn from multilayered tissue paper. 'For making tea. Antique…we've shared so many tea breaks together…we thought it would always remind you of us…'

'I love it.' I hugged them both. I really did love the gleam of the old brass and the curved handle of the teapot resting on the ornate stand. 'It's perfect.'

The samovar looked out of place in the ultramodern apartment. I put it on the end of the granite kitchen bench, but Trent complained.

'Can't we get rid of that thing?'

'It's a present,' I said.

'Why couldn't they give money like ordinary people?'

I practised to be a bag lady. The polished stairs to the apartment were difficult. Plastic shopping bags, clarinet case and a backpack, threatening to burst a diversity of groceries, books and musical scores down the slippery slope. Should have used the lift but I needed the exercise. Even pregnant women should be athletic and trim. Just with a basketball bump tucked under their jumpers.

During orchestra practice, cramps began. Helena was conducting. I was sitting in with the woodwind section, Janet with the violins. When I missed the entry for the clarinets, Helena tapped her baton and we began again. Frowning, she led us at a sprightly tempo through the first movement, but as I leant forward in pain the year ten girl beside me raised her hand and said, 'Excuse me, miss, Mrs Novak is ill.' A fuss ensued that only adolescent girls can produce. An ambulance ride, a seepage of blood on my clothes, and an ultrasound that revealed no little heartbeat. The blessed oblivion of anaesthetic.

*

I accept Trent's kiss on the cheek calmly, wondering what innovative laundry process has resulted in these comprehensive multidirectional creases in his electric-blue T-shirt? He stays for half an hour fiddling with his bike helmet then dashes off for a ten-kilometre ride. Marooned in this white starched hospital bed, anchored to an aluminium intravenous drip stand by metres of plastic tubing, I am safely contained but drifting, drifting in mind and body, flowing away and out and down, oozing from every pore and orifice, my spirit, my self, slipping quietly away.

Evening darkens and the meal tray arrives but the reheated casserole doesn't tempt me. Stars appear in the dark blue velvet above the office blocks and I say a prayer for the lost child, the non-child, the little life that never was. The life that I was building around her is now washed away, drained away with the blood on the white tiled floor as I showered, a worried nurse hovering behind the shower curtain. The meal tray also holds a mandarin. I break open the skin and am surprised by a pool of tart, sweet juice. The segments are gone in a few pungent mouthfuls. I lick the juice from the sour pith-lined shell and wish I hadn't spoilt the sensation.

After two days, I leave Trent's stiff arrangement of banksias and waratahs in the hospital. I tuck the posy of pink rosebuds from Janet and Helena into my overnight bag with my soiled nightdress. Discharged, I'm not waiting for visiting time. Trent is teaching all day; I'll be home first. My taxi drives the long way around the city to the riverside apartment. I get out a block from home and walk. Past empty shopfronts, used bookstores and a pawnshop. Dust and dead leaves swirl in small circles and sparrows peck the mosaic floor of the café in the laneway.

Our new sofa has been delivered – still in the soft plastic wrapping like a dry-cleaned red boomerang. It is in perfect placement in front of the windows overlooking the Yarra. Wind gusts chase heavy clouds across the sky in rapid succession, changing the reflected light from glimpses of gold to solemn grey and back in a matter of seconds. A cream shag-pile rug is carefully parallel to the sofa, and the wall unit at right angles to the suite gleams below the row of Trent's chrome-framed drawings.

Keys in hand I stand, unable to sit on the pristine furniture, appreciating the clean, uncluttered lines but repelled, strangely alienated, by the red leather. Pausing beneath the drawings, I notice for the first time the cross-sectioned cocoon exposing the mysteries of the chrysalis. I pull my coat closer around my body and shiver. I calculate the cost of airfare to Samoa. There is not much in my bank account, and my parents' wedding cheque is already deposited in our new joint account. Trent keeps the chequebook in his briefcase.

I take down the drawing of the sliced cocoon with surgical precision, and lug it down the lift and along the road to the pawn shop. I hurry back to the stillness of the apartment. I load my clarinet, the brass samovar and my passport into Trent's canvas holdall and pick up a suitcase of summer clothes never unpacked since moving. The taxi ride to the airport is swift. No flights to Samoa, but I can get on an evening flight to Fiji. Anywhere warm will do. I leave my overcoat in the transit lounge. I phone Helena and Janet and tell them not to worry. I'll write to Trent…from somewhere warm.

On the Bus

Her Madonna face, creamy skin and luscious curve of lip are all coloured by a purple welt that creeps up over her neck, chin, cheek and brow. She has wound a floral scarf around her dark hair, covering the bruising around her ears. Her neck, emerging from a drawn-up collar, is studded with tiny dark moles like small jet beads sewn to embellish an ivory satin evening bag. She holds her head erect: calm, proud, quiet.

To her chest, she has strapped a baby carrier: and the infant inside is sleeping, downy head held by her mother's gentle hand, when the bus rattles over potholes. There is a toddler, too: dozing in a stroller, dummy in his mouth, flannelette blankie clutched to his heart. He wears faded cotton pyjamas with steam trains on a pale green background. Like the trains, the boy is travelling, and will keep on travelling, around bends and through dark tunnels, into the unknown. His mother has not packed any clothes for him. All she has brought is the baby change bag. She has made it look as though they are just out for a walk, a stroll to the park, or a quick trip to the corner shop for milk.

She has not brought a handbag, keys or wallet. She has an anonymous transport card loaded with credit; cash tucked into her nursing bra, more inside both her sneakers. This money has been saved over weeks and months, little by little, then augmented by pawning her rings, her watch, and the gold earrings she always wears. She flushed the pawn tickets down the toilet in the shopping centre, when she bought small cartons of long-life milk and juice to keep the toddler hydrated on the trip. She will make do with tap water and adrenalin.

She wears cotton trousers and a nondescript shirt. She has boarded a bus that will take her far from the city centre to an outlying suburb she has never seen. There, she will board a train that will take them north through coastal towns and the deep, dangerous night. In the middle of a northern country town, she will find a charity shop, and buy a set of second-hand clothes for each of them. She will change in the community centre toilets, rip up their old clothes and use them to wash the children's sticky faces, bit by bit, leaving the used-up rags of their old life in rubbish bins around the country as she travels.

She will buy nappies, nail scissors and peroxide at a discount chemist. She will take a bus to a smaller town, rent a cheap room in a run-down motel for one night only. They will bathe with scented soap and wrap their pale flesh in clean towels. While the children sleep, she will hack off her long black tresses and bleach the spiky crop left on her scalp. The toddler will be frightened when he wakes: she must wrap her head again in the floral scarf.

In the morning, she will order a large breakfast and feed the toddler up with toast and egg. The baby sucks contentedly at her breast. They will check out minutes before the allotted time, will not risk another night.

Someone has left a pair of sunglasses in a bedside drawer. She will wear them as she boards another bus that will take them across the state boarder. At another charity shop, she will buy a tote bag, a red plastic train for the boy and a baby blanket. She will also purchase a tie-dyed sundress.

They will eat ice cream in a seaside park beneath tall pines. She will push the toddler on the swing. At nightfall, she will trudge the laden stroller over sandy, rubble-coated roads to the women's refuge in a side-street behind a stone church. She will tell a version of her story to the social worker, only one essential part of which is true: she feared for her life, and had to get away.

Cockatoo Pie

You have to make your own opportunities. Maud discovered this essential truth when she was a mere twelve years of age. A father who didn't comeback from Gallipoli; six younger brothers farmed out to relatives; an asthmatic mother working as a maid-of-all-work in the local pub. Only Maud, the eldest, was allowed to stay with her mother in a hotel back bedroom in exchange for skivvying in the kitchen after school. Scrubbing pots. Peeling potatoes. Rolling pastry for pies.

Maud's father hadn't left much to remember him by. A thin gold wedding ring that her mother still wore. A war medal. A suit of newish clothes sold to a travelling salesman to pay for Maud's boots. She couldn't work barefoot in the kitchen, Gus the publican said. Their farm had been on rented land, and their livestock and furniture were sold off to pay debts. Maud possessed her boots, a tattered exercise book in which she practised her copperplate handwriting (much praised by the teacher of the local one-room school), and her father's rifle. The gun was hidden under her bed with a box of bullets. Her mother turned a blind eye to this. *Who knows when a girl might need to defend herself?* Maud had always been a crack shot, better than the boys, when aiming for tin cans or rabbits in the back paddock. Gus paid her cash for fresh meat.

If Maud's two top talents were handwriting and shooting, pastry-making was a close third. Better than bald Reggie, the pub cook, better than her mother – Maud seemed to have the knack of kneading the dough to just the right consistency. Of rolling and prinking and baking to a golden perfection. Sweet and savoury pies graced the hotel table and warmed the bellies of locals and travellers alike. Returning salesmen remembered and asked for the speciality of the house. If beef or mutton were scarce, rabbit could be substituted in the rich brown gravy. If rabbits were hunted out, kangaroo could be slow cooked until tender enough for the table. But if you wanted something really out of the ordinary, you waited for the day when Maud produced her legendary cockatoo pie.

It was old Auntie Esme's recipe. Auntie Esme, whose bark hut by the shallow river was closely guarded by a lanky golden mutt of mixed parentage, would sit in the shade of her mulga tree weaving reed baskets with quick brown fingers. Although she didn't often speak to them, the town kids knew that her dark eyes took in every push, shove and secret liaison on their meandering way home from school. Auntie didn't miss a thing.

It was a hot summer Saturday when Maud went with her gun for rabbits, but having no luck, in frustration took aim at a row of white cockatoos bobbing their yellow-crested heads on the horizontal branch of a ghost gum. She picked them off as easy as pie. When she went to the base of the tree, Auntie Esme was there, shaking her mop of dark hair so that grey streaks glinted silver-white in the sun. For the first time, Maud noticed the sulphur-yellow feathers woven into the dillybag that Auntie carried around her wrist.

Maud kicked at one of the lifeless birds, leaving red dust on the white feathers.

'Show some respect, girl,' Esme chided. 'Take a life, you must make good use of your kill.'

'Useless old cockies,' Maud grumbled. 'Stringy as rope. Reggie tried cooking one once. It got caught in his rabbit trap. No one could force the meat down. Can't get any money for them – Gus only pays me for rabbit or roo.'

Auntie Esme shook her head. 'Gotta know how,' she muttered. She spat out the wad of leaves she had been chewing. 'I'll show ya.'

The old woman gathered the fallen birds and carried them by a string looped around their sad necks. Their yellow crests bounced with each slow step towards town. She walked along the riverbank, stopping now and then to add a frond of fragrant leaves or a handful of pepper-berries to the coolamon balanced on her hip. Maud trailed sullenly behind.

When they reached the pub, Auntie Esme walked in as if she owned the place.

Men drinking in the bar raised their eyebrows, but Gus took no notice. Esme went straight to the kitchen and ferreted about for pots and pans.

'If Auntie Esme is willing to cook for us, I'm first in line with my plate,' Gus told Reggie, who came, grimy cloth in hand, to complain. 'She worked for those rich beggars up on the hill in the old gold rush days. They had an imported Frenchie chef. He taught her all his fancy tricks. Let her be.'

Maud watched as Auntie Esme rooted around in the kitchen to find a large iron pot with a tight lid. Auntie helped herself to the entire stash of lard in the cool room, which she put to melt in the pot. She plucked the birds, swiftly beheaded them with a cleaver, and removed their internal organs. She laid the prepared birds reverently in the molten fat. With her gathered herbs crushed and sprinkled on the top, she lidded the pot and placed it in the oven.

She inspected the wood fire below. 'Not too hot,' she told Maud. 'Leave them there all day, all night.'

Maud noticed that the yellow feather-crests had been removed from the cockatoo heads. Auntie Esme threw the bald heads into the oven fire.

The old woman sat on the back steps, twirling string in her strong fingers, interweaving feathers into a round, oval shape that steadily grew as the hours passed. In the cooling evening, Gus took her a tankard of ale.

In the morning, Maud went to the kitchen and the old woman was still there, stirring a rich vegetable gravy.

'Watch out – steam hot,' she warned, taking the iron pot from the oven, lifting the lid, filling the air with peppery fragrance. Auntie Esme spooned out the cockatoo meat that slid easily from the slender bones, and added it to the broth. 'Better get going on yer pastry,' she said.

That was the first cockatoo pie Maud ever served. Gus paid her double. Auntie Esme left with a sack full of bulky shapes. On the kitchen table she left a dilly bag for Maud, into which were woven white feathers. It was finished with a gathering string tied with a yellow tassel that bounced when you carried the bag on your wrist. Reggie wouldn't allow 'that dirty abo thing' in the kitchen. Maud's asthmatic mother was uneasy at the sight of it. To please her mother, Maud secretly hung it high on a rafter in the washhouse.

Maud had a good memory and could reproduce the pie recipe without any help. But she wrote down the steps, in careful copperplate writing, in her battered exercise book.

The reputation of Maud's cockatoo pie spread like a bush legend, embellished by proud locals and carried far and wide by the men travelling from town to town, searching for work in tough times.

Reggie was jealous. He asked Maud to show him the recipe, but she guarded her secret. When she discovered that Reggie had been searching her belongings, she tore out the recipe from the exercise book and hid it in her dillybag. Gus was on her side: he made sure Reggie was always needed somewhere else, for butchering or carting supplies, on the days she cooked her cockatoo pies.

Years passed. Maud still shared the bedroom with her mother. No longer trekking the dusty track each day to the local school, she helped wash linen and clean dishes at the pub but did not work on the bar.

'I want better for you, Maudie,' her mother sighed, over the endless piles of soaking linen.

Most young men had left town looking for work, and not many of Maud's old classmates were left. The girls Maud had gossiped with between arithmetic problems and recitation were helping at home, walking out with farmers' sons and embroidering teacloths for their hope chests. Maud's hopes were less tangible. Gun over her shoulder, stalking dry paddocks searching for game, she might get a glimpse of colour on the horizon that stirred up restless thoughts in her chest. Most times this was easily quietened by a wordless hour sitting a small distance away from Auntie Esme's hut on the riverbank.

On Sundays, Maud and her mother put on clean blouses and walked to the small timber church used by the Methodists and Presbyterians week about. They weren't fussy about which week it was. Maud enjoyed the Methodist hymns, but the Presbyterian minister was of a literary bent, and was as likely to spout long lines of poetry as verses of scripture. His words becalmed the congregation as if with a lullaby. Maud's weary mother often slept. Maud enjoyed the coolness of the smooth cedar pews and the chance to sit still and embroider her daydreams with threads of silver and sunshine yellow.

Other women were stand-offish to them – working in a hotel, not attending temperance rallies – but the Methodist minister's wife, whose hands inside her tight white gloves were every bit as chaffed and reddened as Maud's mother's, always had a kind word. Before the upheaval of married life and widowhood, the two women had been friends. Once in a while, Maud's mother would walk through the dusk, and rest on a cane chair on the manse veranda, sipping tea with her friend.

When Maud turned seventeen, Reggie proposed marriage. Maud laughed in his face. Tension in the kitchen grew. Pots bubbled ferociously on the fuel stove, bread burned in the oven and milk in the cool room curdled. Maud's mother observed the rough way Reggie bumped into Maud on the stairs, the way his eyes followed her every move, his brazen drooling leer as she crossed the yard to the washhouse.

'I'm not scared of Reggie, Mum,' Maud said. 'Any rate, I have my gun handy.'

The day Reggie grasped Maud's shoulders and pinned her to the wall, pressing his stained apron-clad form against Maud's furious body, her mother took action. Whatever happened next, the situation could not end well.

From that day on, each evening Maud walked down the main street with the minister's wife and slept on a camp bed on the closed-in side veranda of the Methodist manse.

Peppertrees swayed in hot dry winds and the river shrank to a series of brown puddles. Flocks of white-feathered birds flew into her dreams in the arid summer nights. She often woke to the crack of thunder, but the promised rainstorm never arrived.

Gus lost his pub in a fearsome blaze. It went up like a dry haystack in a lightning strike. People said that the jealous cook had been up all night trying to replicate the famous cockatoo pie, but had overloaded the fuel range and made the fat so hot that it caught fire. Reggie, dozing by the oven with a bottle of beer, hadn't the patience or skill of Auntie Esme or the knowledge imparted to Maud. His charred skull was officially identified by the police, his gold tooth a mere molten nugget in his jaw.

Travellers staying in the pub were woken by Gus, frantically ringing the courtyard bell. People stumbled out, choking with smoke, half-naked or in their night clothes – but nothing was saved, not Maud's rifle, or her bullets, or her exercise book.

Maud's mother, part-deaf and in a deep sleep, didn't emerge from the burning building. After the funeral, Maud left town in a second-hand hat provided by the Methodist minister's wife. On her wrist, she carried a dilly bag with a yellow-feathered tassel that bounced as she walked to the train station. In it was a selection of leaf fronds, pepper-berries, and a page torn from her exercise book, covered in careful copperplate.

There would be other kitchens in which to cook cockatoo pie.

The Bangalong Trees

On the road to Meershaum Vale, in a gully just before the last rise, two large fig trees entwine with each other, growing out of the creek that trickles through the land once farmed by a soldier-settler. This man returned from the Great War with a missing right foot, but his wife had waited faithfully and there was a brood of eight children – six strapping sons and two capable country daughters – able to sow the fields and milk the cows, and do their father's bidding in every little whim. He called the homestead Bangalong, in deference to a local Aboriginal word no white man really remembered or understood, but made a joke of it, saying, 'Oh, we bang along all right at our place, one way or another.'

The old man was an expert fiddler, in demand across the countryside for dances and weddings, so often he and his wife rode out in the sulky to gatherings near and far. The children would take advantage of their parents' absence and picnic by the creek: lark about in the shallow waters fishing for yabbies, wrestle each other on the rock ledges and stir the bull ant nests until the angry insects emerged into the daylight, only to be stomped on by well-worn boots.

Other evenings when the old folks were at home, you would hear the strings echo the familiar melody of a hymn across the paddocks in counterpoint to the chirping cicadas. Wild finches, honeyeaters, bower birds and kookaburras listened and accepted the man's singing strings into their bush symphony. Wallabies would pause in the twilight, ears cocked to the sound of the old violin.

It was a great sorrow that all six sons perished in the next war. The daughters too, went as nurses, married and never returned. They settled in southern cities with their veteran husbands and wore rosemary on their lapels each Anzac Day, marching dry-eyed for the memory of the brothers they had lost. The old man and his wife battled on alone, eventually leasing the farm to a neighbour and keeping only a small vegetable patch, a single cow and some chooks for their own needs.

One day late in summer, a lanky-limbed youth tramped up the weedy track from the road with a laden pack on his back and a battered guitar case in his hand. He laid his burdens on the patched wooden boards of the veranda. Knocking on the faded green fretwork of the fly-screen door, he called, 'Hi, Grandma! It's Keith.'

'Dad, it's Lorna's boy!' shouted the old woman, and she began immediately to fuss over her only grandchild. She fetched new-laid eggs, fired up the fuel stove and began to cook as she had in the old days, when there had been the appetites of hard-working men to feed. In the chook pen, the rooster crowed until sunset.

Keith had left university after one undistinguished year. He hung around with the peace protestors, playing folk songs in cafés at night, until the draft was inevitable and it seemed wise to make himself scarce. As the Vietnam war claimed his old schoolmates, he looked up his grandparents in his mother's dog-eared address book, left her a note and hitchhiked north. His grandparents, glad to deprive the war machine of the last of their line, called him John (which was no effort because one of his dead uncles had been John, and he looked quite like him) and told neighbours he was a student from agricultural college come to work in the holidays.

Under his grandfather's supervision, Keith spent his days fighting lantana instead of Asian soldiers. He mended the ramshackle chook house for his grandma and scared off the diamond python that had been stealing chicks. He grew brown and muscled with physical labour, sunshine and his grandma's country cooking. He bought a second-hand motor bike from someone he met in the pub and rode around the property. Sometimes he took a day off to ride east to the sea, but mostly he stayed and made himself useful. On mild evenings, the youth strummed his guitar and the old man reached with arthritic fingers for his bow, and together they stumbled through tunes they both knew.

When the old man died that winter of pneumonia, Keith reminded his grandma that the chooks needed to be fed, that she still needed to eat and drink and go about the business of living. So she got through that time, and he stayed on, took back the land that had been leased out and planted avocado and macadamia trees. 'Bush nuts!' scoffed his Grandma, but she had to admit that the farm began to pay, and there was money for new tools, machinery and a recliner chair that Keith placed near the front window for her, to watch the occasional traffic coming along the country road.

Visitors came for Keith, long-haired boys and girls in their twenties, enjoying a prolonged childhood. They skinny-dipped in the creek and sunned themselves beside the lofty tree ferns. Young women shrieked at the sight of snakes and were bravely defended by their boyfriends. All of them learnt to keep their sandals on and watch for the bull ants that inhabited the rocky land around the creek. But mostly they didn't stay long – Keith was bored with their perpetual games and took the farm work seriously. None of his friends cared to stay and lend a hand.

A more lasting presence was the dark-eyed, brown-skinned girl who worked weekends in the local pub, whose silent barefoot steps meant that you never heard her arrive. She and Keith would walk down to the creek in the evening, or sit on the steps talking softly while the cicadas hummed in the background.

'One of Black Jimmy's mob,' Grandma muttered.

'Her name is Maree,' Keith said. 'Remember, Grandma? *Red and yellow, black and white, all are precious in His sight…*'

The old woman went into the kitchen and started banging around with saucepans and mashing potatoes with a force that made the old kitchen shudder. Her disapproval kept the girl from entering the house, but Maree continued to show up on the veranda, and there was really nothing Grandma could do but sniff loudly and go to bed early.

On the day Keith went off with the tractor and came back towing a dilapidated caravan up the hill, Grandma knew her objections counted for nothing. Maree lived in the caravan, and Keith continued to eat meals at the house. His grandma relied on a sudden onset of deafness to ignore the night-time wanderings of her grandson.

When the old lady took to her bed and didn't get up even to feed the chooks, and the doctor began to visit daily, Maree made herself scarce. Keith sent word to the south. The Bangalong sisters came home, at long last. Lorna and Pearl each left a score of meals in their freezers for their spouses and travelled home to farewell their mother. It was a family reunion long overdue. The daughters cooked, cleaned and cleared the farmhouse even as their mother drew her last breath in the iron-framed bed given her as a wedding present more than half a century ago.

The will was straightforward – half of the property to each sister. Keith offered to stay and manage the farm for them, assuring a profit to their investment, but no, 'Better to sell and leave the past well behind,' they said.

'Time you came home and faced the music,' said Keith's mother.

Keith stood on the veranda listening to the dense silence of the bush. The sounds of his grandfather's fiddle music seemed to echo over the ridge.

'One last walk around the property, for old time's sake,' said the sisters, 'and we'll leave in the morning. Got to get home to Norm and Len,' they said. The sisters found clean handkerchiefs and, tucking the embroidered squares in their sleeves, went arm in arm for their last walk.

The cicadas chanted. The bull ants hurried over the rocks. The kookaburras laughed until the full moon began to rise in the solemn sky. The wallabies paused in their evening grazing, and the bandicoots stopped grubbing for roots in the undergrowth and took cover.

Keith began to throw his gear hastily into his backpack, but the sounds of the night called through the open window, and he heard a soft 'Coo-ee' echo across the yard. He tossed his gear back into the wardrobe and called. Maree came to the door and with a sudden decisive movement he pulled her by the hand into the house and into his bedroom. An hour later, Maree slipped out, but the caravan windows remained dark, and the glow of a campfire could be seen down by the creek.

Keith took a roll of twine and his grandfather's old wooden handled axe and went to the creek. He chopped and bound up an armful of fig tree roots, all the while softly chanting in time with the cicadas. A dark barefoot figure danced, and the shadowy tree ferns lifted their fronds in the light of the campfire as they had in ancient days. Keith threw the tree roots on the fire. A green haze hovered low over the shallow creek waters. Bull ants emerged in great numbers from their tunnels below the rocks and feasted on a fallen fledgling currawong. The night was still and airless. The diamond python slivered unseen across the deserted farmyard to the chook pen.

At daylight, Keith went back to the farmhouse alone. His mother and his aunt were nowhere to be found.

It was easy to bury the two small tartan overnight cases in the field he ploughed that morning. It was easy for the dark-eyed girl to convince the police constable that the women had been driven to the railway station and caught the Sydney-bound train early that morning. It was easy to find a handful of locals in the pub to confirm the departure of the women on the early train.

It was less easy to explain the sudden appearance of two mature fig trees, branches entwined as if they had been there fifty years, beside the creek below the homestead.

Ruby's Piano

'I polished it,' declared Ruby proudly. 'It looks as good as new, don't it, Dad?'

Before even touching the lopsided, upright piano, listing on a broken wheel that had been pushed too roughly over the woolshed floor, I knew it would be hopelessly out of tune. But there was no doubt that Ruby had done her level best: the burled walnut lid shone, reflecting my doubtful smile above my brave, red, polka-dot bowtie. In the absence of a piano stool, two metal chairs had been stacked together to achieve the required height for a pianist. I sat on this impromptu wobbly tower and opened the piano lid, displaying the yellowed ivory keys that looked for all the world like a shearer's shy nicotine-stained smile.

Would the keys be stiff, or so loose that they lacked the necessary punch to reach the strings and make any worthwhile sound? Would all the strings be tautly intact or would there be broken strings and dead notes I would need to avoid? I hesitated, coughing into my handkerchief, rubbing my cold fingers, regretting the financial need that led me to accept this job.

The local dance committee waited around me in an expectant semicircle. A hired musician, I was expected to give value for money, put on a show.

In these minutes of indecision, through the crack between the highest key and the piano's timber end I saw a glimpse of ruby red. Someone has been poking foil chocolate wrappers into the old instrument, I mused. Had Ruby also cleaned the inside? Was she the chocolate eater?

'Any tea in that pot?' I asked, gesturing to the remains of their lunch on a bare trestle table to the side of the temporary stage.

Green velvet curtains were swagged to the side with sprays of wattle and gold ribbon to hide moth holes in the ancient fabric. Despite having been cleaned to within an inch of its life, the shed still smelt of dust and wool and kerosene. An itch in my throat from pollen-laden spring flowers threatened to explode into sneezes. And they think a musician's life is an easy one, I muttered internally. A little breeze moved through the louvre windows high up on the side walls; double doors stood open at the opposite end of the wall from the stage.

Ruby's father spat into a potted palm that was strategically placed to hide a crack in the wall at the back of the stage. 'Get the man some tea, Ruby,' he ordered.

'Yes, Dad.' Ruby scuttled away to find a clean cup.

I made a show of polishing my glasses. People drifted off, disappointed at the lack of a private preview. Ruby brought a thick, pink cup of strong tea, not very hot, and a buttered scone. She placed them on top of the piano and left. There came the sounds of truck motors starting up, voices calling goodbye, and then just the squawk of cockatoos as evening began to fall. The organising committee had gone home to wash and dress in their finery. I was alone. My fingers, greasy from the scone, hovered over the keyboard, but still I did not press a note. My throat, eased by the tea, hummed a line or two of a popular song.

A swift stride over the boards announced the arrival of the fiddler. He shook my hand, which I hastily wiped on my trouser leg, said his name was Bill. In a trice, his instrument was out of its case, and he was tuning, plucking notes, reaching across my body to strike chords on the piano. The old thing had some sound in it, after all. 'Give me an A, Fred,' he said. (Although my name is Frank.) Soon we were playing the standard tunes, any missing melody notes on the piano covered by the fiddle. If I played octaves in the bass, and we avoided B flats, we were all right. The out-of-tune piano had a lopsided, carnivalesque sound. Muted, as if by fog. I thought about opening the top of the piano to investigate, but Ruby returned, in a tiered creation of blue beribboned lace, and replaced my empty cup with a large floral arrangement of wattle and flannel flowers.

'Not bad for an instrument stood out in the paddock for a year,' commented Ruby's dad.

'Dad, I want lessons,' said Ruby defiantly.

'We'll talk about that after Christmas,' he replied. 'When you've finished that dressmaking certificate.'

Ruby twirled, a blue spiral of pleasure.

'Gentleman's washroom outside to the right,' he said. 'You've got twenty minutes until the punters arrive.'

Turns out there was an icebox laden with beer outside beside the gents: this accounted for the regular line of blokes out there beside the dunny. The ladies' refreshment team inside the dance were only serving sandwiches, cake and tea.

We got through the first two sets well enough. The dancers were happy: barn danced, waltzed and quickstepped their way around the vibrating floor enthusiastically. Couples formed and exchanged partners. Sweaty palms slid over frilled shoulders, around sashes on waists. The flowers on the piano top vibrated with sound. The fiddler brought two bottles of beer inside and hid them in his swag behind the piano. Now and then, he passed me a drink in a teacup.

It was all going fine and dandy until an imposing matron with an orchid on her satin-covered bosom made her stately way through the throng and thrust her sheet music into my hands. A bloody soloist. No one had mentioned her. The fiddler and the dancers sat down for a rest. Not the poor piano player, oh no.

The songs were old-fashioned, sentimental, not challenging. I appointed Ruby page-turner: told her to turn the page on my nod. I strummed the opening chords of the song, which unfortunately was in the key of F: the soloist pulled a face at me when the B flat vibrated weakly on a totally different pitch, but turned a smile to the audience, and began. With one hand dramatically placed on the piano, she stood and opened her capacious lungs. The piano performed less well without the violin to supply missing notes. The soloist sang on regardless, darting glances at me as if it were my fault when a dodgy note jarred or a blank space in an arpeggio left a beat of silence when none was expected.

'I am used to working with PROFESSIONALS!' she hissed at me under her breath as she left the stage to exuberant applause.

The fiddler bounced up with a refilled cup and we were off again with a foxtrot, and everyone was happy, except for the poor piano player who badly needed to pee.

A Scottish reel was requested, and I left the fiddler to cope with that on his own. Some joker with a mouth organ jumped up on the stage to join in. I made my escape to the gents and relieved my bladder with a long sigh. I rinsed my face in cold water from an outside tap, wiped it with a handkerchief sewn with my initials. I turned to go back inside, but there was Ruby, with a slice of rainbow cake on a plate.

'You must be hungry,' she said. 'You do play wonderful! Try this. Made it myself.'

I took the plate and gulped a fork full. 'Was the piano really out in a paddock?' I asked.

'Yes, sir. It was out in the paddock ever since my mumma left with a salesman on the railway. Dad don't want no memory of her in the house. But we had no rain since before she left, so it's still dry, no mould nor nothing.'

'That's sad. How old are you, Ruby?'

'Fifteen. Will you learn me to play that piano? Show me a little? So Dad will let me bring it inside.'

'Sure.'

We went inside and I showed her some chords and how to find middle C. Her father arrived on stage, and sent Ruby off to help with the refreshments, while the paid musicians earned our fees. We bashed our way through a repeat of the first set, the pace getting more and more frantic as the fiddler gained speed like a racehorse in sight of the finish line.

The soloist was brought back to the stage by a group of encouraging women. 'Auld Lang Syne,' said the lady to me, smiling as if all were forgiven. 'They want to finish with Auld Lang Syne.'

The fiddler stayed to help this time, and we managed a beautiful ending between the three of us. I almost shed a tear. The fiddler actually planted a kiss right on the pouting mouth of the singer, in the pause before she took her bow. Ruby ran up to present her with the native flowers that had rested all night, quivering to the music, on the old piano top. As the soloist bowed, I saw a little black star shape crawl from the wattle onto her cleavage. The spot of red on the shiny black spider was unmistakable. I froze in horror. I looked again at the crack at the treble end of the piano, and saw again the ruby dot shining in the harsh electric light. I jumped up to fling open the piano, and saw a mire of thick, webbed white across the full width of the strings and hammers. No wonder the sound was muted. Mother redback and all her sisters, aunties and cousins had been laying eggs in there all the year-long, and now they were awake with the noise.

Unbelievably, the soloist had not yet seen the spider on her bosom, not yet felt the fangs slide poison into her skin. I didn't know how to save her, and even if I had, would I have intervened?

'Encore!' the crowd called. 'Encore!'

With the piano innards still open to the air, I sat myself back on the wobbly chairs, and cascaded an inviting arpeggio up and down the keys. The fiddler quietly encased his violin and left the stage. I saw him accept an envelope from Ruby's father and disappear into the night

'Ruby!' I hissed, as the soloist began the first verse of an Irish air, 'Ruby…ask your dad for my pay now, will you? I'll need to get away in a hurry to catch my train.'

Dream Desk

It was the desk I had always wanted. Rich red mahogany that had never seen the bristles of any misguided renovator's paintbrush, or the ravages of a paint-stripping acid bath – it glowed with patina after of years of use. The original brass handles, blackened with age, remained on eight wide, deep drawers. The last item in a job lot from a deceased estate auction, it was being unloaded from the delivery truck.

'What about this one, boss?' The driver wiped the sweat from his forehead with the back of a hand blackened with dust and grime. 'Out on the spare parts heap?'

'I'll give you forty dollars,' I interrupted.

The dealer squinted at me through narrow eyes and held a folded newspaper over his bald head against the midday sun. 'Nice timber in it,' he muttered. 'South American mahogany. Fifty.'

Driving home along Windsor Road, I wondered how I would get the desk out of the four-wheel drive by myself, let alone up the steps to my second-floor unit. How would I transform the useless junk shop purchase into a functional piece? Because although the desk was complete, whole and beautiful in my imagination, in reality it was useless. Across the top of the desk, a jagged, gaping wound of splintered timber split the surface completely asunder. As a writing desk, it was a lemon.

The phone was ringing as I opened the door to the unit.

'Just ringing to say thank you for this morning,' wavered my mother's voice. 'It was so good to have a car to do the shopping, and get all those specials. I wouldn't have been able to carry the lemonade on the bus.'

'No worries,' I said. 'Got to go, there's someone at the door,' and I wasn't lying, there really was someone tapping on the windowpane beside the open door. My mother didn't know I had been loitering in the antique shops after kissing her goodbye at eleven a.m., groceries unpacked, in her retirement village.

'Saw you drive in,' said my neighbour Brian. 'There's no power in the units. It's been off for about an hour.'

'Thanks.' I threw down my keys and bag that I had still been holding. 'Like a cup of tea?' I gave Brian a full-faced smile.

'What about the hot water?'

'Never mind about that,' I cooed. 'I've got gas.'

Over tea and gingernuts, I told my neighbour about my morning's shopping, and invited him out to see the desk. Brian produced a heavy-duty trolley from his garage and manhandled the desk out of the four-wheel drive, up the stairs and into my unit before the tea leaves were cold. It wasn't really that difficult; after all it was essentially in two pieces. The clumsy iron bracket holding the pieces together snapped off as Brian pulled it from the van.

I gave Brian more tea. The desk stood like an injured animal; pieces propped together in the middle of my tiny living room. I wasn't sorry to hurry him out. I really did have a three o'clock appointment. I threw a dust sheet over the desk and hurried to the hairdresser.

'Not working today?' asked the chirpy hairdresser between the foils.

'No, it's my flexi day,' I replied, wiping a drip about to reach my eye.

'Oh, luverly. Wish I had those. Do you have one every Friday? Been shopping?'

'No. Yes. I took my mother grocery shopping. She's eighty-two, can't get about much, so I've been out to Windsor and back this morning to drive her.'

There's a lull in the conversation while she folds a difficult strand of hair.

'Have you got children?'

The inevitable question. 'Yes,' I say. 'A son. But he's travelling overseas.'

This is my standard line. I never go into details. The eight-year search for this missing boy, brilliant at school and the joy of our lives, inexplicably lost in a foreign country. The loss that destroyed my marriage and haunts every waking moment. My former husband travels the same territory in South America over and over but finds no trace of him. I have learnt to carry the deep ache like a familiar black handbag, worn and misshapen, that can never be thrown away.

'Going out tonight?' comes the next query.

'Yes.' I can answer this one truthfully. 'I'm going out to dinner.'

'Well, your hair is going to look really nice,' the girl says, swathing my head in a black towel. 'Coffee?'

*

Lingering over our empty wine glasses, Paul and I decline the dessert menu but are in no hurry to leave. Our evenings together always follow the same pattern.

'I'm flying to Singapore in the morning.'

'Conference?'

'Just a routine visit, I'll be back Monday night.'

Paul travels constantly as a sales manager. I make no effort to keep up with the details of his life. He knows little of mine. We see each other now and then – no strings. Light and impersonal – no questions asked.

'Early flight?'

'Six-thirty.'

'Better make a move then.'

*

Paul closed the front door of my unit at two a.m. and, as I listened to his quiet footsteps fading down the stairs, I weighed up the probability of being able to sleep. Active thoughts piloted my bone-tired body to the bathroom. I ran a scented bath and soaked by candlelight. Still no electricity.

In my towelling robe, I lit the gas to warm some milk, hoping to induce a few hours' sleep. Waiting for the milk to heat, I remembered the desk. With a tug, I attempted to pull the dust sheet off, but it stuck. Probably snagged on the splintery surface, I thought, so I pulled harder and lost my balance. I fell, hitting my head heavily on the floor. Still holding the corner of the sheet, I felt myself being pulled along, as if into a dark tunnel of mossy green. From a distance, I could hear the hissing of the stove and the burnt smell of milk bubbling over…but I had travelled too far to do anything about it…

My feet are sodden in mouldy hiking boots and my hand reaches for muddy vines rising from swampy ground. Slipping and struggling up a hill covered in unrecognisable vegetation, I ignore the rustlings of who knows what in the undergrowth. Anything to reach the top. Desperate for air and sunlight. Parrots screech and flap technicolour wings in my face. A slow coil of snakeskin is visible between the ferns. I'm making progress, but then I slip, my ladder of tangled vines falls apart in my hands and, as I am swallowed by huge reptilian jaws, I hear my angel's voice: *Mum, I'm coming. Hold on, Mum!*

'Do you want me to call your mum? The ambulance is coming.' Brian is shaking my arm, wrapping a blanket over my shivering limbs. 'What happened? I smelt the smoke. You should have a smoke alarm, you know. Could have burnt down the whole building. Had to force your front door, but I'll fix it in the morning. Are you all right?'

The ambulance officers came, but I convinced them I was OK. They dressed the cut on my head and Brian fussed, cleaning the stove and making me sip sweet tea. I huddled on the sofa, hardly moving from my nest of blankets the entire weekend, cosseted by my attentive neighbour. I dozed and I wrote, furtively, in my dream journal, when Brian was in the kitchen, or out buying treats.

On Sunday, he laid the desk on the floor, brought power tools and cut away the splintered middle section. He sanded and planed, apologised about the mess, and bolted the two pieces together with a brass plate covering the join. 'Not beautiful, but functional,' he said.

'It's perfect, Brian,' I replied. 'Thanks.'

On Monday night, finally alone, I showered and dressed and made up my face. I took furniture polish and stroked the desk in slow, meditative circles. I manoeuvred it into the alcove beside the window. I lubricated the drawer runners with candle wax. Polished the drawer handles and fetched a key from my old oak wardrobe. It fitted the locks on the drawers perfectly. From under my bed, I collected a pile of used notebooks. I slid these dream journals, their pages lined with silent explanations, into the mahogany drawers. One for each of the empty years. I locked them and hung the key on a gold chain with my wedding ring.

Then I drove to the airport to meet Paul.

In a Circular Motion

Janelle peered into the barrel of the heavy-duty, ten-kilogram Whirlpool washing machine, big enough to wash the entire team's football jerseys in one load. It was always a challenge to reach down into the bottom of the barrel to find the last item, without a stool to stand on or a borrowed arm from a passing teenager to reach the dregs of the wash, the last sock or pair of patterned boxers. Now, of course, there was never anyone passing by at the right time. Dave went to golf early, before she put on the first load. Why she still washed every day was a question she did not care to ask herself. It was a ritual, the putting on of the washer while she brewed a second cup of tea to sip while she scanned the morning paper. Towels on Friday, sheets on Saturday, Dave's golfing clothes on Sunday when he did not play; Monday, tea towels and anything of hers worn on the weekend that needed doing; Tuesday more of Dave's golf shirts and smelly socks. Wednesday there was always the odd beach towel or tablecloth to do; Thursday the dog's blanket often took a turn and emerged from the tumble-drier fluffed and ready to cuddle Henry the cocker-spaniel's arthritic legs. There always seemed to be something to wash, something in the dirty clothes basket, even with all four children married and gone.

She tugged the corner of Dave's blue-checked shirt, shook it free from the tangled mess in the barrel of the washer – how did there manage to be so much in the wash on a Tuesday? – but found herself holding Amy's short-skirted primary school uniform of green plaid. She closed her eyes and threw the offending garment in to the kitchen tidy. She left the rest of the wet clothes in the washing machine and went out.

Janelle ironed on Wednesdays. It was just what she did. The hump in the week, the halfway day, was one she had always tried to keep free to catch up with domestic chores, even when teaching. She marked the midpoint of the week with a long session of bad daytime TV and the fragrance of Fabulon, making tidy piles of freshly ironed linen.

Janelle lifted the next item from her ironing pile and thought, how did this get here? Peter's brown shirt? When he had left home months ago? But she deftly ironed it and then set it aside in the spare wardrobe, with a pile of clothes waiting to go to St Vincent de Paul.

Thursday was a fine day, perfect for sitting on the veranda with a cuppa, scratching Henry behind the ears, waiting for the wash to finish spinning.

'I didn't put that in the washing machine! Truly, I didn't!' She cried aloud in frustration. But there, large as life, was the chocolate-brown shirt once again, the one she had bought for Peter to wear for work experience in year ten, from Target, and that he had worn to all his part-time jobs. It had worn so well, she could not help thinking, for a cheap brand.

She plucked Dave's Christmas gift cartoon character sock from a twist of T-shirts and pillowcases, hung Goofy on the line with a green plastic peg, and searched the intertwined pieces of wet fabric for its mate – that bit of yellow must certainly be it, she thought, tugging the fragment, extricating not a sock but the yellow satin binding of the bunny rug with which she had swaddled her first born child.

It must be dementia, she thought. I must be putting these things in the wash and forgetting I did it. There is no other explanation. But where am I finding them? Surely, they were all thrown away years ago?

To prove her sanity, she resisted the urge to toss the entire contents of the washing basket into the incinerator and fling in a lighted match; no, she would calmly and carefully hang each item, no matter how upsetting the memory and bizarre the effect, side by side on the Hills hoist and wind up the line to spin and dry beautifully in the sun and fresh air.

She went inside to make coffee and, while sipping decaffeinated Nescafé, phoned to make an appointment with her GP. She found the sudoku book Dave had been given for Christmas with the Goofy socks, and did five pages before lunch. Mental exercise, physical exercise…she recalled. These preventative measures had been listed in the magazine article about preventing Alzheimer's disease. Dave would be home soon.

She would make a light salad for lunch.

Janelle really didn't mind having Dave around, now that he had retired. He played golf twice a week, sometimes more; did the grocery shopping, was full of projects. He didn't follow her around like a lost sheep the way some retired husbands are said to. It was just like a long school holiday, really. Dave had been principal of the local high school for ten years; a head teacher before that. He was involved with many community groups and was in demand for more. He would have to go back to work for a rest, he joked. There was also his book that he would not talk about, that he wrote in the newly papered den that had been Peter's room. Janelle suspected he spent a lot of his writing time dozing or polishing his golf clubs. But whatever he did, in his den with the door closed, was his business. As was her personal retreat, created from another empty bedroom. Their renovated Californian bungalow was spacious, and had an upstairs extension which was their master suite. Even with the luxury of a study each, there was a spare room for visitors, should it be needed. I still have to clear out the wardrobe in Dave's den, Janelle sighed. Still, there was no rush. It could wait for another day.

Janelle had been a teacher, too – music was her subject – part-time after the children were born, casual in later years. She was still on the lists, would get a call sometimes to babysit a year nine class whose teacher had been driven to distraction by their adolescent antics, or to cover for someone on maternity leave. She usually said no, particularly since Dave had retired. The calls had become less frequent, and now she didn't even bother keeping a bag of standby lesson materials packed and handy.

More than eight years ago, Amy had married, moved out of her front bedroom with the lead-lighted bay window and provided Janelle with the spare room she craved. With her part-time earnings, Janelle had purchased a new piano, recovered a sofa in cheerful chintz and lined the walls with her books. She went into the room now and looked at the dust on the closed piano lid. How long since she played? Not that the piano was really her instrument, it was just one of the tools of the music teacher's trade. No, her talent had been the voice, and singing her love. Longer, even, since she had sung or conducted a choir.

A couple of overseas trips she and Dave had taken in the first enthusiasm of his retirement had seen her cancel the private pupils she had taken on. She hadn't bothered to revive the activity. There was always something else to do.

She sat at the piano and opened the lid. Began a few scales up and down the keyboard. This is good for the brain too, she told herself. And Mozart. Must find that book of Mozart sonatas. But later. A sense of fatigue washed over her. She decided on a wee lie down before Dave got home.

'Mmm, you smell nice,' said Dave as he nuzzled her neck. He was fresh from the shower, home from golf, and Janelle had been deeply asleep.

Janelle has a book club friend who prefers the type of romantic novel where any suggestion of physical intimacy between story characters is represented by a certain amount of curtain fluttering at the bedroom window. Suffice it to say that Janelle's bedroom curtains are fluttering in a very strong breeze at this point in our story.

Once the wind had died down, Dave kissed Janelle on the shoulder and said, 'I'm hungry. Why don't we drive to the point for fish and chips?'

Janelle remembered her good intentions and ordered a side salad with her beer-battered flathead and fries. Sitting on the wharf beneath a market umbrella with a chilled glass of sav blanc in hand, she confessed. 'Dave, I think I'm losing it.'

'That's good. The diet's working, then?'

'NO! Dave.' Janelle administered a swift kick to Dave's ankles. 'I think I'm getting Alzheimer's.'

'Why? That's absurd.'

'I'm doing strange things.'

'Menopause.'

'No. That was ages ago.'

'Oh.'

'I'm losing my mind.'

'You are NOT losing your mind. Have some more wine.'

Friday morning, Dave had a committee meeting at the local council chambers at nine. Janelle did her usual routine of throwing the bath towels into the wash before breakfast. Nothing sinister about these large apricot rectangles, she thought. Nothing mysterious here. She did not even LOOK in the dirty clothes basket, but averted her eyes as she passed by, arms full of towels.

Nonchalantly, she opened the washing machine an hour later after completing a soothing crossword. Cryptic. All spaces neatly completed. She stretched out her fingers like crab's claws and hooked a piece of fabric lurking in the edge of the barrel. She pulled out a pink Bonds Grosuit. Such as Amy had worn twenty-five years ago as an infant. 'This is truly the last straw,' Janelle cried inwardly, holding on to the rim of the washing machine to maintain her balance. She closed her eyes, put the lot into the tumble drier and went to lie down.

After a week of denial and avoidance, Janelle decided to stop throwing the unwanted, reappearing laundry items into the bin, a corner of the laundry or the compost heap. She had decided to embrace her madness in full view of *Dr Phil*. As she ironed, she methodically hung each dress and shirt on a rail she kept for this purpose; made neat piles of folded linen and pressed shorts. So, after Dave's shirts, the tea towels and pillowcases, her sky-blue linen shirt and white Capri's, she carefully and expertly ironed the bunny rug, the school uniform, the soccer shorts, the chocolate-brown shirt (again). Baby Grosuits do not need ironing. They are wash and wear, simply bouncing back into shape, even after all this time. She folded the pink arms and legs neatly, did up all the little press studs along the front, and placed it on top of the pile, grinning at *Dr Phil*. She was on the last tiny T-shirt, patterned with giraffes, when Dave came home.

'What are you ironing that for?' he asked. 'No need to iron dusters. Or wash them, really. There are plenty more in the ragbag.'

'…ragbag…?'

'The ragbag in the wardrobe in my den. You said if I needed a rag for washing the car or polishing my golf clubs, look in the ragbag.'

'…but…'

'I know you've been feeling a bit lost lately, but honey, ironing dusters is going a bit far…'

Dave was lucky Janelle was not a violent woman, or else he would have worn the steam iron around his ears.

'You mean you've been putting them in the washing machine?'

'Yes. You're always on at me about recycling.'

'Dave, you are the limit. I thought I was going mad. Why didn't you tell me?'

'Tell you what?'

'Never mind. No, don't sit down. Carry this pile. I'll get the rest from the den. We're taking the lot to St Vinnie's. Right now. I've had quite enough of these clothes going round in circles.'

No Stones

She nearly walked straight into him, coming around the street corner, walking purposefully on the narrow footpath, he just closing the gate in the low white picket fence, still showing the tidemark of recent floods.

Their simultaneous apologies, in broken half-sentences, were polite and automatic.

You're Tom's wife, aren't you?

She was startled to hear her husband's name slide so glibly from a stranger's tongue.

How did you…

How do I know Tom? We often have a chat or walk to the station together. And I've heard you talking.

Yes. OK. Got to rush.

She knew this man by sight; recognised his square, well-shaven jaw. His short-cut, spiky, optimistic hair. The too-careful, almost childlike presentation of his well-ironed shirt, the knife crease in his pants.

Tom hasn't been around much lately. Is he away?

No. Have to…

Oh, don't go! The fingers of his left hand grazed the thin cotton over her right nipple. She suddenly understood the purpose of his Coke-bottle glasses, the loosely held white cane.

Sorry, she said. And felt obligated somehow, by his downcast face, to explain. Tom never came home. After the floods. OK? He never came home. I don't know where he is, or which sodden veranda of which stinking house his corpse is rotting under. I just don't know.

She stood, motionless, emptied of this information, emptied of life.

This time, his fingers found her arm, held it, above her elbow, stroked it upwards, patted her shoulder. She did not pull away. Was strangely reassured by the touch of his warm, dry hand on her shivering skin.

Why don't you come in? He opened the gate and led her up the steps, across the splintery veranda and opened the screen door. The front door he unlocked with a key on a chain which he deftly pulled from his pocket.

You weren't flooded, then? she asked politely.

No, these old Queenslanders are built high enough. My grandad knew what he was about.

She looked around and saw the furniture, a mix of old and new, sentimental and practical. A new computer with various peripherals spread over an oak dining table in the middle of the room. Without asking, he boiled the kettle and made two mugs of instant coffee.

You live alone?

Yes. Dad died eight years ago.

I'm sorry.

He had a good innings. Sorry about Tom. No one tells me the local gossip. I mean the local news. I'm well informed on international affairs, though, he quipped.

She sipped the coffee. Too sweet, but hot.

You knew Tom, you said?

Yes. We often walked from the station together.

He never said.

Were you flooded out?

Just downstairs. Not that bad. Car ruined.

And Tom?

Went out to help, never came home.

They'll find him.

But he won't be alive, will he, after all this time?

There was no answer to that, even for a resourceful blind man, so they sat in silence as the light dimmed, afternoon shadows lengthening, the sunset moving higher up the patterned wall with a rose-shaded glow.

After a while, she put her feet up on the vinyl couch and rested her head on the square arm rest.

Later, when she woke, she had been covered by a crocheted rug, such as your grandmother might have stitched, in long-past days. There was a moth hole in it, and she poked her pinkie through, idly, as she remembered how she came to be in this unfamiliar place.

I cooked, he said. Do you like sausages?

Not hungry, she said. I'll be going now.

She let herself out the front door, opened the gate in the picket fence, and walked to the river, where swollen banks still throbbed with unusual force, and wildlife had deserted the normally tranquil reed-ponds and mangroves. She thought of Virginia Woolf, but could find no stones.

Waiting

As I unlock the past, little by little, scene by scene, doorway by doorway, it is the small, forgotten things that surprise me the most. How you caught me unawares that day as I hung out the twins' washing, on the sagging clothes line between the weathered, silver-timbered clothes props – caught me by the waist and danced a waltz on uneven ground peppered with rabbit holes – oh yes, the little moments, long buried in time and forgetfulness, like dried lavender at the bottom of the lingerie drawer, folded between faded silk nightgowns not worn since my long-gone honeymoon.

The sun glinted in the spaces between the washed linen and glanced off your glasses. Four-eyes, the men called you to your face, other things behind your back, that I wasn't supposed to hear. Old four-eyes, but those blue eyes, protected by thick lenses, saw most things. Too many things. Too many things I would rather have kept unseen. You saw into my life and my lack of happiness. Not unhappiness – for that is surely an active emotion, reacting against injustice, circumstance or suffering – no, my lack of happiness was more a numbness of spirit, a lack of beauty and ex-perience in the humdrum consequences of my life choices. Not that we thought we had any real choices, in those days. Today, I would probably be diagnosed with depression and be given medication. In those days, there was no help but the domination of the capable, tough old bird who was my mother-in-law, and the indifference of the man who was my husband.

But you saw. You saw the person me, and danced her around the wicker basket loaded with sodden sheets, round and around the dying lettuces in the vegetable patch and into the paddock.

She watched us, that old woman my mother-in-law, and reported to her son.

'Dancing in the field.'

'Neglecting those babies.'

'Can't stir a pot of soup without scalding the pan.' Another sip of her steaming black tea passed her thin, wrinkled lips.

And he listened, that husband of mine, who drank his tea quickly, eager to get back to the shearing shed, the paddock, where he was boss. The house was women's work, and if I didn't rule it as I ought, he looked to the old despot, his mother, to bake the bread.

The bread was baked every Monday. Loaves and loaves of pale, mounded dough put to prove under chequered teacloths. The smell of the yeast made me ill – early in my marriage when I was newly expecting, I was released from this duty by the shearer's cook. Not you, an earlier edition. She drank, though, and when the bottles were found broken and smashed about the kitchen after an early binge one Monday, glass even in the bread dough, she had to be dismissed. There were few cooks to be found, but after months of layabouts and tired, travelling families looking for work, somehow you arrived, took charge, and all was well.

I didn't mind being in the kitchen after that, watching the way your clever hands pounded dough and kneaded pastry, sliced warm mutton and peeled potatoes in one continuous curl of brown skin. A circle of calm grew around you, and all I had to do was relax into it. Your hands, strong, firm and quick, as they rubbed butter and flour together in the oversized mixing bowl. So many scones for so many hungry shearers. Mine had always been like cobblestones. How did I manage to scorch the edges and yet find the centres uncooked? No one was sorry when you arrived to take over the kitchen, in the months I rested, after giving birth. Even the twins were entranced. They settled so much better within the radius of your smile as I rocked them in the double pram after a feed.

The last time I saw your hands, they swung an overstuffed duffel-bag into the tray of your ute, then wiped the dust and sweat on your hips, patting the fat wallet full of cash my husband had paid you, in lieu of finishing the month, to see the back of your interfering ways.

You didn't turn and wave – you didn't speak or make any sign. That was how I knew, I knew, I had not seen the last of you.

And I'm waiting. Still waiting, after all this time. Oh, my love.

You drove too fast for safety down the dust-blown track between straggly melaleucas. The windbreak line of English oaks, planted along the drive, had not yet taken off. Spindly, sticklike saplings with brown spotted leaves, they marked the road into the property. I told Robert he should pull them out.

That line of English oaks either side of the gravel drive, decades later, are now in fresh, green leaf. Solid, deep-rooted trees, they haven't been touched by bushfire or pestilence. I wander beneath their shade sometimes, of a summer evening, and kick my toes against the protruding roots, crack a dry acorn still lying on the ground from last autumn. You have been lost to me, but will arrive one day, as suddenly as you departed, and those purposeful hands will cradle my face between them and look once more, deep into the reality of me. And I will know, at last, who I am.

There has been war and fighting, sorrow and disease, but I have outlived Robert, his iron-faced mother and even my poor, self-sufficient twin sons. I mourned them, of course I did. I was that much of a mother at least, at the tragedy and the waste of it. No other children had been born to me and Robert. Not that I didn't do my wifely duty, as required – full of submission and meekness. Perhaps it was my lack of ardour that caused the marriage to sour like grapes on a withered vine – or perhaps there had never really been any love at all. There has been war and sorrow – but still I wait for you. I linger in the shadow of the oak trees and wait for a sign of dust clouds rising from the unsealed road you must travel on to find me here. Waiting, as I always will, as I must. They tell me I must sell up, leave the property and move somewhere close to town. But how can I leave this place, when it is the only way you will find me? I hold tight to a branch of oak and close my eyes to see your face.

Today I wake, from a dream of you, and wonder what all the fuss had been about. If you had simply kissed my face, and pulled my body across the void to lean on the weight of yours. If you had discovered my breasts with your mouth and run your hands over the curve of my back, just once, we might have known, for good and all, if it was merely a trick of the mind or an impulse of the body – we were both already long past any vague thoughts about the meeting of souls.

But you didn't – and I, meekly, held to principles of faith and fidelity so tightly that both of us are now left with this unopened Pandora's box, full of monsters and untasted delights, visions and wonderings, that once in a while surface in dreams, or lift a faceless head in the dark hours after midnight, to drag us back into the turmoil of past desire, and leave us wondering what might have been. At least, I do, dear. I wonder about your peace of mind, about the distance your body has traversed in these years when my hair has silvered to pure white, and the full breasts you might have loved, have dwindled in despair. Oh, my love.

But you never were. I never dared call you that. Even in dreams, you were never mine.

It's a grey morning outside my bedroom window, this familiar dusty pane of wood-framed glass, draped with torn and ragged lace. I know where the cobwebs gather, and I know how many weeks may pass before they are so noticeable, they must be swept away with the dusting broom. The sky is heavy with moisture, but not heavy enough to release a downpour. I know mornings like this; there have been so many – days of unfulfilled promise, skies of portent that never deliver the longed-for storm. This waiting, patient world I inhabit, where nothing occurs, and the summer thunderstorm wheels around to the right, missing this drought-dry property altogether and showering other, more blessed and worthy neighbours, with precious rain.

It will not rain here, today. I am sure of it.

Your Middle Name

The second-hand shop is so crowded your eye cannot take it all in. Small china cats, porcelain teacups, souvenir snow globes, all so close together in wall-to-wall glass cases forming a visual collage of pre-loved tat. A *Where's Wally* for the collector. You come back often, to feed your obsession, always noticing something new, something previously overlooked; some little thing that is the current object of your fervent desire.

You point, with one extended finger, at the small treasure you now need beyond all else.

The shopkeeper raises a quizzical eyebrow as if to say 'Really? You want to pay money for THAT?' But takes it from the case, reads out the handwritten price ticket, takes your coins, wraps the treasure in recycled newsprint, or used bubble-wrap, or a brand-name carry bag from a long-ago fashion trend.

You leave the shop, elated to be the new Keeper of the Holy Grail. You unwrap it, throw away the tatty wrapping. Wash your purchase gently in soapy water, polish with a clean cotton cloth, examining for crazing, chips. Identify the maker's mark, make a space in your cabinet, place the tiny china figure beside all the others. Lock the door with satisfaction.

Next day, you are back at the second-hand shop poring over the glass cases, once more scanning for a find.

You realise things are getting out of hand the day you purchase a duplicate figure, not realising until you get it home that its twin is already on your shelf. Thus begins a passion for creating pairs that gives your display cabinets a certain pleasing symmetry, lovely to behold.

The second-hand shop is not your only source of supply, but it is your favourite. The shopkeeper – with her broken taped-up spectacles and her gentle, rolling walk – allows you to put items aside for payday, will occasionally point out new items in the three-dimensional collage that is her life's work. She tells her assistant to give you a chipped, worthless Cupid for free, as you eye it greedily. She feeds your habit. She knows your middle name.

It is desire.

Hopes and Fears

A slow hot morning, a mixed-up sort of day: a quick lunch break in the snowflake-decorated library café so I can leave early this afternoon; a bunch of visiting children and their mothers singing songs about reindeer, making crêpe paper snowmen and listening to the nativity story in the children's reading room; a couple of harassed students studying for late exams; pensioners borrowing large-print detective novels and wanting extended due dates to cover them over the holiday shutdown; someone wants to know the population of Brazil – then I am asked for a Bible.

Like all good librarians, I know my collection well, and know exactly where it is on the reference shelf. Go straight there, take it down, feel the solid weight of good paper inside cloth-covered boards in my competent hands.

It opens, like an eagle's wings ready for flight, in a V-shape, at the place where a royal blue ribbon marks the beginning of Psalm 23. The book was last used at Harry's memorial service. He died suddenly, at work, of a heart attack. There is a tree planted outside the library in his memory, with a plaque; the director read from the psalm as we gathered around the sapling in a minute's silence. Some people were uneasy about the Bible being read; although the shepherd psalm is surely the most comforting and uncontroversial of passages, unlikely to raise the ire of atheist or people of other faiths.

Today, the Bible requester is a teacher, who wants to check a name, a verse – an evangelical student has submitted an essay in which she has tried to convert the teacher with a fundamentalist reiteration of various quotes and misquotes. The teacher, brought up in the Anglican tradition, wants to make a correct and suitable reply.

I suggest a verse from Micah, am proclaimed a marvel – all in a day's work for an educated librarian, I reflect.

I can name the books of the Bible in order, like a religious alphabet; I know how to open the Bible volume in half and half again by the width of the closed pages to find where the drama of the New Testament begins, after the buffering bulk of the old. The Bible drills of my protestant childhood and the tunes of Sunday school songs are forever lodged in my memory.

I do not regret those childhood hours, but am grateful for the knowledge I carry in my fingertips, even though I no longer help fill a pew and bow my head each Sunday. There were worse ways to spend a weekend morning. I do not think the computer game players and TV-watchers of the current generation are any better off.

It used to be that in every library created for public, student or professional use, there would be a core group of reference tools – including a Bible, a dictionary, (Oxford if the library could afford it), and a set of encyclopaedias, usually *Britannica*. The holy trinity of reference work. Those were the days when real people asked you proper questions, humbly, and with suitable gratitude for your swift, accurate answers. These days, everyone Googles, and believes everything they read on Wikipedia. Heaven help us.

In my library before last, in a small vocational college, bursting at the seams with computer manuals, office procedures and cookbooks, I installed a new row of smart, Colourbond steel shelving, taller than usual and fixed to the wall for safety, where I moved the reference books so that the burgeoning borrowing collection could expand into their old rows. It so happened that the Bible, high up on the first, top shelf, was now in full view of the front door.

It can be that the library Bible gathers dust all year, year after year, untouched except for the annual dusting at stocktake time, then it is put back neatly in place, when lesser items such as the monthly newsletter of the computer-users group might be justly deemed obsolete, and duly discarded.

Along with the computing tomes and illustrated guides to the correct preparation of shellfish, in that library we also had travel books and English language learning materials. A good section of the college community were migrants, newly arrived, or women still struggling with our language after decades of isolation in their homes, relying on their integrated children to interpret for them, trying to learn English from TV watching, now being pushed by their naturalised Australian children into mixing with the wider community, and learning to read and write the language of their adopted country. You could tell these families, the women were often driven to school by solemn looking, silver-haired men, who stood in the car park, leaning against the bonnet of their Mercedes or Jag, smoking while waiting for their wives to finish class; they preferred that the teacher be a woman, and the other students all women too. Just occasionally, one of the men would be persuaded to attend class with his wife – and other women would suddenly become reserved and less able to participate: as if a curtain had been brought down on the rising sun of their learning.

Not long after my new reference shelves were installed, one of these men came into the library and handed me a book.

'You have a Bible,' he said, pointing to the top shelf. 'You also need our holy book.' He left.

I opened the gilt-edged volume he had placed on the counter, and found it was a Qur'an.

It was quiet, that day, in the library. I had plenty of time to record the details of the donation in the register, consult my cataloguing tools and create a bibliographic record for the Qur'an. I printed a spine label with a call number, covered the book in protective plastic film and stamped the library ownership mark on the title page. I placed the book on the reference shelf in correct call number order, pleased with my timely and efficient work, acceptance of multiculturalism and productive afternoon.

Next day, the silver-haired man was back. I proudly indicated the Qur'an on the shelf.

'No!' he objected. 'You have put it on a lower shelf than your Bible. It should be of the same importance.'

I was immediately reminded of the scene in the musical *The King and I*, where no subject of the king was allowed to stand if the king sat, the head of the king always needing to be the highest in the land.

This is absurd, I thought.

I showed the man the spine labels. I took out my copy of the *Dewey Decimal Classification* scheme (abridged version for small libraries) and showed him the pages where the Bible and the Qur'an were allocated specific numbers. I showed him that I had followed the rules explicitly, my insistent finger emphasizing the numbers on the spines of the books, which have, incidentally, filed the Qur'an on the shelf below the Bible.

The man left, shaking his head.

For a moment, I considered changing the call numbers, to place the books side by side. Who would notice the classification error but me? (But how would I decide which came first, the Bible or the Qur'an? Wouldn't the donor then insist that the Qur'an be first?) I decided to leave my work alone. I wondered how many other holy books I might have to deal with, and checked the ones Dewey listed. The classification system is such a nineteenth-century dinosaur in its attempt to chart all knowledge. Full of prejudices. Just like Wikipedia, really.

I sighed at the list of religions and sacred literatures. Should I go out and purchase them all? That was a question for the college director at the next library committee meeting. I did not have enough funding to cover it. Perhaps community groups would all donate their religious literature.

In the end, it didn't matter: government funding cuts closed the college, dispersed the neat library I had presided over. I don't know what happened to the Bible or the Qur'an: I left for my next job before the hammer fell. I never saw the silver-haired man again.

I am roused from these memories by a junior colleague relieving me from desk duty, so that I have time to complete some bibliographic checking at my workroom desk before leaving early as planned. There are community carols tonight, and I am a tenor in the choir. I love those old hymns, the four-part harmony, the orchestra backing and the precision demanded by the conductor. It is the highlight of my year. I pack up and walk through car park to my second-hand Mazda. I turn on the radio news, and hear the clipped tones of the radio announcer report a wave of bombing in the Middle East: museums and cultural collections, historic libraries, all destroyed. I picture the fragments of lost words, floating like melting snowflakes in clouds of white ash, scattered over cobbled streets and broken arches. I begin to hum, 'Oh little town of Bethlehem…'

All Souls

Someone died here.

I looked around the room, fresh with new paint, bright with new furniture and modern fittings. *Rubbish. It's a new building. They haven't even finished the landscaping.*

I tell you, someone died here. Isabelle lay on the hospital bed. Although it was discreetly made up with a floral bedspread, the bed was one of the few indicators of what this room was. She leant up and fiddled with the buttons above the headboard.

You're imagining things.

I tell you, someone…

Now you've pressed the nurse call button!

I need to go to the bathroom anyway.

I'd wheeled Isabelle from the car in a borrowed wheelchair. She could still take a few steps unassisted. I hadn't realised going to the bathroom alone presented any problems.

It just exhausts me so, she explained. *I'm better with help – then I'll have a bit of energy left…for visitors.* Isabelle smiled wryly. A young woman in a pleasant green uniform appeared at the door. *Prompt,* Isabelle murmured. *Making a good first impression. Fetch my other bag, will you?*

I left Isabelle with her new carer. Along the corridors of the facility I tiptoed, admiring the new carpets, the tasteful décor, and the savoury smell of the lunch being cooked. If you have to be somewhere like this, you could do much worse. I collected Isabelle's bag from the car, balancing it in one hand and the flowering cactus I'd brought in the other.

I loitered in the foyer to let Isabelle get settled. I picked up a brochure from a stand near the front door and scanned the contents. A series of buildings had stood on this site. Before this new hospice, a 1950s old folks home; a veterans' hostel; a haven for unwed mothers in the 1920s; a grand house of the gold rush days; a colonial bark dwelling. The Aboriginal people of the area got a brief mention. Their word for the local river provided the name. I wondered how accurate the translation was, or if the local tribe had played a joke on the foreigners, giving them a word rude or absurd.

No place is ever free of the past.

Isabelle had lunch in her room on a tray slung across the bed. When I returned from the car, she had changed into pajamas and been tucked into the bed.

I'm tired, she explained. She picked at the casserole, spooned a few mouthfuls of crème brulee into her mouth. Sipped water through a straw. *I'm OK with this*, she said.

With the food?

With dying.

The word had now been uttered. Until now, we'd hedged around it, danced a polite dance to a tune of clichéd optimism, written a whole new thesaurus of synonyms to cover the knowledge we hadn't had the honesty to name.

Nodding was the best I could do. I'd been rearranging the items on the table near the window, deciding where the cactus would get enough light. I came to the chair by the bed, sat down and held the dry, warm hand she offered me.

I stayed through the afternoon, reluctant to leave, reluctant to go home to the empty house with Isabelle's things still everywhere: her paintings, her books, her music. The clothes she hadn't brought with her had been stuffed by her own hands into black garbage bags. I had been forced, by her insistent demands, to deliver them to the op shop clothing bin on our drive to the hospice. She had edited the memories I would have of her. She was still in control.

There was a will, which I simply refused to read, in an official envelope on the mantelpiece at home. I didn't need to read it to know she had left me the house, her money. There might be some distant relatives to make trouble about that down the track. Right now it was the least of my worries.

When the evening meal arrived, Isabelle shooed me away. *Go home,* she ordered. *Get some exercise. Get some food. See you tomorrow.*

She allowed a kiss on her forehead.

I didn't go home, I went to a shopping mall, ate fast food, drank coffee, and went to a movie. By ten-thirty p.m., I was back at her door. I peered in. The lights were off, and Isabelle was sleeping. There was just the gold glow of a nightlight from the bathroom, and the low whir of the air conditioning. I went quietly to the arm chair in the corner. For a while I dozed, exhausted. Around midnight something woke me – not Isabelle, she was sleeping like a lamb. The door seemed to quiver. I closed my eyes. Then there was the sound of muffled footsteps. A nurse doing rounds? I was wide awake.

A queue of transparent forms walked slowly in, as if entering a movie theatre. People of all sizes and shapes, in hats and coats, night-gowns and uniforms, bandages and berets. All made of the same clear, pearly white. They walked in a sociable line through the closed door, across the width of Isabelle's room, and out the fixed glass pane to the balcony. I peered out between the blinds and saw them, all congregated comfortably on the terrace, faces lifted to the moonlight.

Then the transparent shape of Isabelle joined them.

The Passing

The ashes were in a simple box of silky oak. It fitted with room to spare in Mavis's shopping trolley. She placed the worn vinyl tartan thing against the wall in the hallway, ready to go. The trip to the churchyard was manageable on foot, and the priest would be waiting. There would be no other mourners. She directed her attention to dressing the children. Jim was easily caught, instructed to wash and put on his best white shirt.

Oh, Ma, do I have to come?

Show a bit of respect for your dad, boy.

Like he respected me with his belt, often enough.

No cheek, now, Jim. Respect for the dead is called for, no matter what he were in life.

The little ones were playing in the sand heap, and couldn't be called; Mavis had to go right out into the muddy yard, spoiling her fresh stockings on the nettles along the broken fence. She could see Davy holding the edge of a black, flapping thing, Emily cowering under his gesture. As she reached the sand edges of the pile, she could see the furred body of a juvenile flying fox dangling from one extended wing held in Davy's stubby young fingers. The other wing was delicately folded over the bat's chest. His pointy little chin pulled in; the black eyes dull with grains of sand.

Where did you get that thing?

The dog brought it...

Heavens above, throw it away, we'll all be struck down with rabies, boy!

The mechanical notes of 'Greensleeves' crescendoed up the road, signalling the slow passing of the ice cream van.

Mum, can I have an ice cream? asked Emily.

Ice cream. No time for ice cream, girl, time to get ready.

Dad always let me have an ice cream.

Dad's not here and he won't be. Come and get washed, we've a job to do.

I want ice cream!

Dragging a child in each hand, she lugged them into the house, doused them in cold water at the bathroom sink and towelled each small grimy hand with a threadbare towel. The woman she saw in the cracked, spotted mirror above the sink was no one she recognised. *How did I get so hard-looking?* she wondered. Mavis took up the stiff-bristled brush and tidied the hair of each child, not ungently.

Pausing by the front door she pulled a beaten-up leather purse from the shopping trolley and took the last two shillings from its crumby depths. She called to Jim, *Go get four ice creams from the truck. Hurry, boy, before it's too late.*

If the priest wouldn't wait, she'd stow the ashes in the churchyard herself.

The Surface of the Wind

Beatrice's coat had a velvet collar. Only the collar – the rest was service-able woollen serge. She wore the blue coat over her gingham dress to church, with shined-up shoes and bleached cotton socks. If the shoes were tight and scuffed under their polish, would anyone look closely enough to care? The veneer was what mattered; appearances were all.

She stroked the velvet with idle fingers as the preacher rambled, losing his congregation in his twisted avenues of thought. Not during the scripture reading, oh no: Beatrice sat upright and all ears for those majestic words rolling off the silver tongue of Mr Boniface, known for prowess in public speaking. No one else ever read the lesson. It was his, and his alone, to intone the magic of the scriptures.

Just as it was Elsie Black's prerogative to pump out hymns, musical or not, on the wheezy organ. Sometimes the dust motes danced with joy at the sounds her fingers produced; at other times the music was dull and tuneless, an ordeal to be battled through, even to the last line of a six-stanza hymn.

Beatrice loved the way Elsie Black swayed with the cadence of the three-fold amen: like a cobra dancing from a woven basket, Elsie's spine twisted and arched into a spasm of ecstasy as she released the final chord.

Beatrice slid unnoticed through the departing crowd, through the gothic doorframe. She went into the copse of birch trees and waited, playing with fallen leaves, or petals drifted from wildflowers in the meadow beyond. The petals were soft and smooth like her collar, but she did not know their name; they were children dressed in their Sunday best for the pleasure of God.

Beatrice is the only child of aged parents. Not their actual flesh and blood, mind; she is the daughter of the local grocer whose wife died in childbirth. 'She's no bother,' her adoptive mother was wont to say. 'No bother at all.

It is a good thing to be no bother, Beatrice knew, when you are living on goodwill in a house where all coins are counted and no one wastes yesterday's stale loaf. It could be lonely, though, without even a cat for company. Is lonely for ever? wondered Beatrice. She half-believed in the goodness of providence to the orphan, in the power of the almighty to deliver her into a paradise of good things.

I shall not be lonely in heaven, she thought. Mother will be there.

Her arms encircled a small birch tree, and she kissed the smooth bark, with lips as red and raw in the cold morning air as cherries boiled in a copper pot for jam.

There is a place. A place where there is milk in abundance. Her foster parents gave her milk, each day one measured cup, never more nor less. She longed for a pitcher of creamy milk to pour and pour and refill the cup, never worry if a drop was spilt, with always some left for the neighbour's cat.

'Where shall we go, and whom shall we ask,' Mr Boniface's velvet voice had intoned, 'when you have the words of eternal life?'

A scented breeze blows petals up from the meadow. They dance around Beatrice's head like the fairies she knows are just stories.

She hears words on the wind, not in the voice of Mr Boniface, but surely one of his kin: 'You touch the ruffled surface of the wind. You smooth the creases of a worried world.'

With a cleansing breath, the air, unsullied by human cells, continues its work.

In Good Company

'We've been waiting for you,' says Christina. 'Rather like goblins.' She smiles a gentle smile.

Her hair, drawn back from the serious forehead, I recognise from her brother's paintings; her calm welcome I accept without question; her gracious leading, I follow. I can't quite conceive how she knows who I am – why she should be waiting to greet me.

Another woman appears at her side.

'Here's Elizabeth,' says Christina. 'Your other welcomer.'

'Come to the poet's room,' says Elizabeth. 'Judith and Emily are waiting. Judith is particularly anxious to greet another Aussie.' This slang word slips rather strangely from the tongue of this Victorian lady.

'You are surprised,' she commented, 'that I know the lingo. We don't stagnate here, you know. We are all up to date. We know what's been happening in the world. Robert is quite enamoured with rap. Although I must say, postmodernism does not appeal to us at all.'

'We are so looking forward to hearing your poems,' says Christina. 'Your reading is scheduled for tomorrow, right after Bashō and Wang Wei.'

'…my…reading?' I gulp. *Is this heaven or hell?* I wonder.

'Yes, of course. All newcomers are scheduled to read their work as soon as they're settled in. You must not deprive us of your words.'

'We won't monopolise you, of course,' adds Elizabeth. 'The novelists are waiting to meet you too.' She guides me to a book-lined room where a glowing fire radiates warmth and light.

Chopin plays a waltz on a grand piano in the adjacent ballroom. Through the arched, open doorway, curtained with rich velvet and scarlet silk, I can see a group of people in various styles of dress listening attentively. John Donne chats with Rumi; Sappho taps her foot as William Blake gestures in the air. A pair of dancers, feet clad in ballet slippers, dance on the elegant parquet floor. Chopin (*Chopin!*) lifts his eyes to me and graciously nods to acknowledge my presence. The dancers twirl and I feel faint.

Elizabeth guides me to a wing-backed chair near the fire. A bearded gent bows and offers me a down pillow for my back. (How does he know about my sciatica?) Although I must say that it is not painful at all today.

'Thanks, Will,' says Christina. To me she adds, 'Such a gentleman, our Will Shakespeare. He has had such a calming influence on Sylvia.' A woman, dressed in apparel evidently from the 1960s, takes Shakespeare by the hand and leads him to the ballroom where they begin to waltz.

I close my eyes and wonder when I will wake.

A cup of fragrant tea is placed on a small table near my elbow. 'This will help,' says an Australian voice. 'It is normal to feel a bit disoriented at first.'

I know this woman from her photograph. I turn and face Judith Wright full on to say thank you.

'It's all right,' Judith assures me. 'I'm not deaf here. You will find that all your aches and pains are gone. Some people still wear their glasses as an affectation, which of course is up to them. But I was only too happy to throw mine, and my hearing aids, out the window.' She sits companionably on an ottoman in front of the fire. 'Feeling better?' she asks.

'So I am really here…this is really it…I mean, we are in…?'

'In heaven?' she laughs. 'Yes. Heaven for poets, writers, artists, readers…all in this precinct. The sportsmen have a different pavilion, the mathematicians and scientists too. There is a bit of heaven for everyone.'

I look around nervously. 'And…where is He?'

'You were expecting a gilt throne and a voice of judgement?'

'Well…'

'He dwells with us as he has always done,' Judith replies. 'In and amongst us. In our words and in our deeds.'

'Will I see him…?'

'You want to know if you will see God?' asks Judith. She points to the pen and paper I hadn't seen before on the table beside me. 'You will find him in the words he gives you. The artists paint him, the musicians play his melodies. He lives in every breath we take.'

Chopin finishes the waltz and a new music fills the room. A symphonic sound, something I have never heard before. I am entranced; I fall into a dreamlike state and am lifted, it would seem, high into the air and floated into a realm of golden light. I feel welcoming angels all around me, the presence of God in the ineffable holiness of the trance. I drift back to my chair, open my eyes again and smile at the gathered faces.

'You were blessed,' says Christina. She hands me the pen and paper. 'We are longing to read the poem you'll write.'

I take the pen, and words flow without effort, without strain.

I am in heaven.

The Cave

I hadn't expected there would really be a cave.

It was a legend, a family myth, a story Dad told each year around the dinner table when the Christmas trifle was reduced to a creamy blur in Grandma's cut-glass dish. I wonder which sister snaffled that glittery heirloom in the post-funeral bun rush? All Mum's tarnished silver tea-spoons, green depression-glass dishes, vintage enamel cookware with chipped edges, all piled in cardboard boxes, stowed quickly into the back of the hatchback or the four-wheel drive. They left me just the basic Woollies-bought everyday stuff. I'd been living here on my own for so long, Mum in the nursing home, it was a wonder my sisters hadn't taken all her good stuff ages ago. It was their right, it seemed, to plunder the kitchen – I had been given all Dad's naval memorabilia at his death, ten years ago. This was their turn.

Beans. While the girls were looting the kitchen cupboards, they dis-covered my cache of baked beans. Rows of tins – I buy them by the carton at the bulk grocery outlet in Wanganoo, along with oversized tins of dog food for Brent – stacked three high on the pantry shelves.

'My God, Graham!' called Celia. 'Don't you eat anything but beans?'

'You really need to take better care of yourself than that,' said Kay. 'None of us are getting any younger. Fresh foods, wholegrains…'

'Nothing wrong with beans,' I said, dodging out the door.

'Do you think he's going a bit…funny…living by himself?' Celia asked, as I retreated across the lawn.

I smiled. Beans are my breakfast staple, that's all. There's a two-dollar roast at the club for lunch or, if they're biting, fresh mullet; bags of tomatoes and huge bunches of silverbeet wrapped in newspaper from neighbours up and down the row of five acre lots on our potholed, un-sealed road.

I don't bother with dairy. Black tea; no cheese – it never did suit my digestion, although Brent loves it when he gets a sliver of tasty cheddar from Norma and Bob next door, while we're sitting over a few ales in the evening. And I have a tin of ginger nuts always full, but that's in my room tucked under the bed, for sucking and dunking in my mug of tea over a late-night read, and the girls, as sure as eggs, *they* won't be allowed to ferret around *in there.*

The tattered screen door bounced and clanged against the door jamb as I walked beachwards, to the growing tide swell that moaned like an injured dog in my half-deaf ears. Brent had woken from his slumber on the couch to follow me.

Past the kiddies kicking beach balls over stumped-up sand; past the wrinkled, tanned diehards on their towels forever sunning their sandy, oiled backs with bikini strings undone; past the surfers beyond the breakers waiting for a decent wave; past the fishermen's eskies and their rods slung out across the tide line from sawn-off lengths of PVC pipe wedged into the sand. Brent lingered and sniffed; he was well known to all the locals. I walked past all these visible signs of humanity. The voices echoed fainter and fainter as the bird calls grew more and more plaintive as I neared the cape.

Normally, I would stand on the headland and watch out to sea, or crouch in a sheltered spot on bare rock if the wind were fierce. Perhaps the funeral had left me with a basic need for shelter but, for whatever reason, today I eschewed the open knoll and climbed down the jagged cliff. I clambered over piles of exposed rocks washed by the sea's relent-less churning, like so many children's blocks tossed by a child-giant into his foaming bath.

The sea was cold on my bare toes. I took off my rubber thongs and tucked them into the back pockets of my baggy khaki shorts, and headed around the point. The tide was leaving, drawing back as every-thing else in my life had a habit of doing. I took my cue from the forces of nature, an opportunist, as always, and began to remember the stories of the cave, embroidered with purple detail at each new telling, deeply engraved on my heart with the weight of childhood belief in a loved adult's words.

My shorts were soaked by the time I was around the corner and could no longer see the long expanse of sand north of the point. Like a woman removing a veil, the tide withdrew inch by inch, until I could plainly see the curvature of the rocks, the tunnel-like entrance to the mysteries of family lore. I hesitated, for who could tell when the tide would return, and I would be lost, trapped or drowned, while seeking nothingness, a fairy tale of an old man's making to bolster his position of authority in the tribal gathering. I plunged into the darkness.

Immediately, I heard a ringing, like a bellbird, but echoing, chiming, resounding with a harmonic effect unlike anything I had ever witnessed. As my eyes became accustomed to the dark, I trod deeper and deeper into a cavern, the sound intensifying. I could just about make out the shapes of boulders on either side. Then I was astounded to see that a light glowed from an inner part of the chamber, leading me through the sand lined tunnel, beckoning, pulsating, in time with the haunting song.

Her eyes, her wistful, strange eyes with the brilliant lapis lazuli irises, drilled into my skull like a speed bore.

She sat on the edge of a wooden dinghy, large gaping hole in its side, lying like a slaughtered whale on the floor of the cave. She was naked – her slender arms, resting by her sides had an olive-green tinge, as did her exposed torso and the buoyant, dark-nippled breasts that bore no resemblance to the coy bosoms of the sunbathers on the beach. Gleaming, Celtic-black hair hung past her waist. She had no feet, no legs, just one muscular tail, not scaled like a fish, but smooth and curved like a dolphin. She raised one arm, grasping a harpoon of ancient design. I could see the glint of the bladed point and barbed hooks that would make retrieval from a bed of flesh impossible.

A leaping blur of wet, brown dog hair crashed through the gloom, landing with a thud that coincided with a shriek of inhuman intensity, and a sudden plunge back into black silence. I heard a crunch of metal on bone and an animalistic sigh of expelled breath, either the dying spirit of the merwoman or my poor Brent.

I turned and stumbled, half crawled, back to the opening of the cave. The waters were knee-deep. I had to hurry back around the rocks to the main beach. When I finally made it up onto dry sand, I saw that my clothes were splattered in red dots that could only be sprayed blood. I wept for my dog.

I sat for a long time, watching the breakers. A sailboat left the cove making swift progress towards the horizon. Two figures paced quickly along the beach. My sisters arrived without speaking, settled either side of me on the sand.

Celia handed me a hanky as Kay said, 'I knew it would wash over you before long, Graham. You can't tell me you aren't grieving.'

I let them fuss over me, couldn't tell them it wasn't Mum I was cry-ing for.

'Sorry, Graham, but there's more bad news,' said Kay. 'Norma and Bob found Brent lying up on the headland. He's in a bad way, lost a lot of blood...'

I was on my feet, stumbling through the churned-over sands.

'Brent doesn't usually go off alone like that, does he?' asked Celia, struggling to keep up. 'Oh look!' she cried, pointing out to sea. 'A dol-phin!'

'Wrong colour for a dolphin,' said Kay. 'Sort of greenish.'

'Must be the light. What else could it be?'

'Dad's mermaid. Remember the story of the mermaid's cave, Gra-ham?'

I was jogging up the slope to the car park, the quickest way home. 'The warrior-mermaid...protecting...her...treasure cave,' I recite be-tween gasps. 'Corrupted by pirates...' I stopped now, hunched, hands on my knees, catching my breath. 'She outlived them all to be sole in-heritor of their sea plunder.'

Wondering what stores of gold sovereigns, pearls and emeralds Brent's canine eyes must have seen on his desperate climb through smugglers' tunnels to the headland, I began running.

Dodging cars entering and leaving the car park, loaded with spear guns and fishing rods; weaving through the flock of red and yellow life-savers packing away their gear in the surf club; jumping the grevillea-edged pathway; cutting across the oval pocked with rabbit holes that Brent loved to sniff and dig.

Sprinting now along the unsealed road, I didn't see the dusty track or the black cockatoo soaring overhead. I saw the lined face of my father, telling his tale, one drooping eyelid covering an empty eye-socket, his one green eye glittering as his booming naval commander's voice declared, 'Nothing else could have saved me, lad – I ripped it from that sea-bitch's finger, and put it in place of my eye…'

I ran straight past Brent where he lay bleeding on the front veranda. Past Dad's stern portrait in the hall, to my childhood bedroom. Pulled the bed roughly from the wall, reached for the suitcase that was pushed right to the back for safekeeping. I cursed the stiff brass buckles on the leather straps, fumbled with the rusty catch. At last the lid was free and I pushed aside old uniforms, medals and maps to find a water-stained calico pouch tied with string. I ran with it, loosening the wrapping with my teeth, finally shaking loose from wads of cotton a heavy, gold-set emerald ring. I laid it in Brent's ragged wound. As Celia and Kay reached the house, the dog took one deep, slow intake of breath. And another.

Going Under

'How's the swimming going, Chick?'

'I don't like swimming, Grandpa.'

'I know you don't, Chick. What's this?' He pulled out the cardboard corner protruding from Anne's bag, resting on the thick slats of the bus stop bench, and read,

Awarded to
Anne Perkins
for proficiency in
dog-paddle
Parramatta Swimming Centre
9th September 1966.

'Well, Chick! You aren't doing so badly.'

'But it's only dog-paddle, Grandpa. To get the next one for real swimming, you have to go *under*.'

'Go under?'

'Under the water. Put your whole face in the water, open your eyes, and blow bubbles. I don't like it, Grandpa. It hurts my eyes. I'll drown.'

'You'll never drown with the teacher and me watching you, Chick. I promise you that.'

Anne snuggled against Grandpa's cotton shirt, ran a finger around a button that was hanging loose from a thread halfway down his chest. 'What did you bring me, Grandpa?' She delved into his shirt pocket. 'Thanks, Grandpa.' Anne kissed the stubble on his chin, began pulling off bits of silver paper from the roll of Lifesavers. 'Where did you learn to swim, Grandpa?'

'Well, now. I didn't have any fancy lessons. Taught meself in the pond. Right muddy it were, after the rain. None of these chlorinated pools in them days.'

'Where was the pond, Grandpa?'

'On my grandpa's farm.' Grandpa's cloudy brown eyes fixed on a point far on the horizon.

'Did you have chickens and ducks?'

'And pigs, and cows…and an orchard of the sweetest apples and pears you ever sank your teeth into – wish I could taste one of those pears again, the ones here are nothing like…'

'Want a Lifesaver, Grandpa?'

They sucked the candies companionably, until the bus arrived.

'Chick.'

'Yes, Grandpa?'

'Chick, I'm going to hospital for a little while.'

'Will you be back for tea, Grandpa?'

'No, I'll be in hospital for a month, so I can't come to see you swim next week.'

'Oh, Grandpa!'

'Now you just keep on swimming, Chick, don't let me down. It's only water, nothing to be afraid of, the same water that makes the grass and the willow trees grow, that you drink and brush your teeth in every morning. I want you to look after my book of poems while I'm gone.'

'The book with the shadow in it?'

'That's the one.'

'When we get home, will you read it for me, Grandpa?'

'Yes, Chick, I'll read it and you shall keep it safe for me, under your pillow.'

Anne was first finished eating her lamb chop and mashed potato, tinned pears and ice cream. 'Pears, Grandpa!' she said.

'Maybe later,' he said, shaking his head at the pale, cold arcs floating in sugar syrup.

Anne was first to leave the crowded kitchen table. She dragged Grandpa to the room she shared with Jenny, the baby, and as the rest of the family fussed around the black and white television set and fought over who would finish the drying up, Grandpa settled himself on the end of Anne's bed. He opened the worn cloth binding with loving hands. Anne stroked the gold letters on this book Grandpa had owned ever since he was a boy, long ago in that far away place called England.

'Tell me what the words say, Grandpa.'

'*A Child's Garden of Verses,* by Robert Louis Stevenson.'

Anne knew the words, of course she did, hadn't they read it so many times before? But she loved the sound of them as Grandpa read in his deep, round voice that was like no other. Anne turned the pages until she found the one she wanted – a picture of a child, a boy, but it looked a lot like Anne, with a shadow looming large and grey against the green, striped, old fashioned wallpaper. Grandpa read,

> I have a little shadow that goes in and out with me,
> And what can be the use of him is more than I can see.
> He is very, very like me from the heels up to the head…

When the poem was finished, they sat quietly for a while.

Anne traced the outline of the gilt apples on the cover with gentle fingertips. She opened the book and stared at the copperplate writing on the flyleaf. 'What does this say, Grandpa?'

'Presented to Thomas Alfred Perkins in recognition of his courage and bravery on this ninth day of September in the Year of our Lord nineteen hundred and ten.'

'Presented to who?'

'That's me, chick.'

'Why?'

'I saved a girl from drowning, a long time ago.' Grandpa kissed Anne's forehead and tucked the book under her pillow. 'Courage, Chick,' he said. 'Time for sleep.'

On Thursday morning, something was up. It was quiet in the kitchen. Anne heard snatches of grownup conversation as she tiptoed down the hall.

'…never came out of the anesthetic.'

'…said he had a weak heart.'

Mum was dabbing her eyes with a bunched up hanky when Anne ventured in. Dad didn't go to work. He left his grey dustcoat and work bag behind the door. He put on a white shirt and tie and solemnly backed the Holden down the drive.

Mum called the children together. 'Dad's upset today, so you children have to be real good.'

'What's up, Mum? Why didn't he go to work?'

'Listen and I'll tell you.' With a quick glance at Anne, she said, 'Grandpa's not coming home from hospital. He's…gone to heaven. Dad's real sad – me too – 'cause we won't see Grandpa any more.'

'Is heaven further than England?' Anne asked.

'Yes, stupid,' said John, the eldest. 'Much further. It means he's dead, Annie-nannie-nanny-goat.'

'John! That's enough,' said Mum. 'Grandpa's gone to heaven, Anne, where he won't be sick any more. But we will be sad, without him.'

'But I'm minding his book of poems! He has to come home!'

'Well, you'll have to keep on minding it, and remember Grandpa when you read it.'

'I don't want the poems, I want Grandpa.' Anne grabbed Mum's gingham housecoat.

Mum shushed the older kids and took Anne and Jenny back to their beds. She brought toast and honey to eat, and told Anne she could stay home from school. Anne felt the hard lump beneath her pillow, and heard the last line of her poem replay over and over: 'Had stayed at home behind me and was fast asleep in bed.'

Somehow life went on. The weather turned cold and miserable. Mum took Anne on the Woodville Road bus once a week to Parramatta for swimming lessons. Without Grandpa, Anne's stomach just felt empty and hollow. She learnt to safety jump from the tiled edge of the intermediate pool, shivering in her wet costume. But when it came to blowing bubbles underwater, the instructor tried cajolery and even threats, but the stinging water was Anne's enemy and she simply refused.

'Stubborn as a nanny goat,' jeered John, when Mum related Anne's fears around the tea table.

Anne ran to her room and cried, holding her book with tight fingers under the pillow.

Next swimming day, they caught an early bus. They browsed the wrought-iron sale tables outside Grace Brothers. Mum bought hot chips and vanilla milkshakes. Anne knew it was meant as a treat, but she couldn't swallow the chips, and every sip of vanilla froth was a struggle to force down her burning throat. The chlorine-soaked air stung Anne's nostrils as they stood in line at the swimming pool turnstiles, waiting to put their coins in the slot. Mum sat with her woven raffia basket, keeping Jenny within arm's length, sending Anne encouraging smiles. After the misery of swimming Anne walked over wet, concrete floors to the change rooms, full of open cubicles where alarming women undressed and pulled dark one piece suits over long bare legs, and slapped white rubber swimming caps over their ears.

On the bus, Anne leant her hot forehead against Mum's cool, bare arm. Jenny, cradled in Mum's lap, cried and pushed Anne away. The ride home was an age of noisy, jolting misery. She lay on the lounge watching TV until teatime. The little she managed to eat came up, an hour later, on the marbled green bathroom floor. Mum tucked her into bed with an Aspro and a glass of water.

The next day, they walked up the steep hill to the doctor.

'Anne has to have her tonsils out,' Mum told Dad when he came home to sip hot tea and read *The Sun* at the kitchen table.

Anne listened from the hallway, then went to her room and pulled the book from under her pillow. 'I have to go to hospital, like you,' Anne whispered.

As she flipped the pages, a photo fell from the book. It was him, she was sure, not Grandpa as she knew him, but as a boy, leaning against a barn door.

'I wish you hadn't gone to heaven, Grandpa.'

*

Mum was sewing dresses for Anne and her sisters on the Elna. A pile of polished cotton print, cut into straight, sleeveless shifts for summer, was being passed beneath the bobbing needle. Anne crept from her bed and stood behind Mum's rickety chair.

'What's the matter, Annie? Feeling sick again?'

Anne shook her head. 'When I go to hospital like Grandpa…'

'Yes?' Mum asked, leaning down to rethread the sewing machine.

'Do I have to go to heaven too?'

Mum turned with a jump and gathered Anne in her freckled arms. She kissed the child's feverish head. 'No, sweetie. You'll stay there for about five days, eating jelly and ice cream, and come home feeling much, much better.'

'So I don't get to see Grandpa?'

'No, Annie.'

*

From the wooden box speakers high on the wall in the children's ward, Dusty Springfield sang, 'You don't have to stay for ever, I will understand.' The polished linoleum was cold on Anne's bare toes.

Sister asked, 'Haven't you any slippers?'

Mum hadn't packed any, although she had redressed Anne's baby doll and bought a new doll's bottle, full of milk that disappeared when tipped to the baby's mouth, then magically reappeared. White-starched headdress flapping, Sister walked a stately progress to the linen cupboard, drew out a pair of too-big, cream-white knitted socks. Anne flapped around in them all day, until it was time.

'How old are you, Anne?'

'Six.'

'Good. Can you count to ten?'

Anne nodded.

125

'Can you do it for me now? Count backwards? From ten?'

'Ten, nine, eight, seven, six, five...'

Falling, Anne is falling, into a deep black space. Not afraid, just falling, muscles loose, limbs relaxed, and then she lands, not on a rock or a bed or a grassy place, but on a hard meniscus of water. A belly flop, a miscalculated dive that stings the ego but sustains no real injury. And she continues to fall, deep, deep into a cold moving stream. Fresh, not chlorinated, water is gurgling in her throat, invading her nose, and when she tentatively opens her eyes it is a green world of weed and re-flected willow branches, high above, that she sees.

Many voices, children's voices, in their high-pitched tones are call-ing, shouting, calling for help.

A familiar voice close by says, 'All right, I've got you, don't worry, keep your face high, soon be out...'

Hoisted up a muddy bank onto long, unmown grass, Anne was propped against a wide tree. She felt the deeply creviced bark scratch her skin where the hospital gown had come untied at the back.

'Am I in heaven?'

'Heavens no!' said a boy in dripping tweed breeches. He flicked water from his face with a swift, practiced movement. 'You're in Hol-loway Farm. What were you doing in the pond, skylarking with no clothes...'

'Who is she, Tom?'

'Never seen her before.'

'What sort of a frock is that? No petticoat, no hose...'

Children in long, heavy dresses and strange boots crowded around. Anne was dazed but unaccountably unafraid.

A woman in a long-skirted outfit and a large brimmed hat pushed through the crowd. The woman slipped a knitted shawl from her shoul-ders and tucked it around Anne for warmth. 'There,' she said kindly. 'I'm Lady Waddell. You aren't one of my Sunday school pupils, are you? What's your name?'

'Anne.'

'Where is your home, child?'

'P…Parramatta.' Anne begins to shiver.

'I'd best take her home to Holloway Hall,' said Lady Waddell. 'She is obviously ill.'

*

'It were a wedding present, weren't it. Thirty year that plate 'as stood on the mantel, an never anyone 'as even eaten off it. And then you goes an' knocks it down into bloomin' smithereens on yer first day at 'ome… why I didn't take a switch to yer ankles like yer da would ha'e done… thirty year that plate. I loved it, reflectin' the firelight of a night. Even the time old puss chased a mouse clear along the mantel, he never knocked it. It takes you not 'alf an hour and me best treasure is ruined. Never find another like it, not after thirty year…'

The voice ranted on, as Anne stood, embarrassed, with Lady Waddell outside the open door. The lady smiled at Anne, coughed loudly, and knocked.

'Oh, Marm, didn't hear you knocking.'

Lady Waddell sat her basket on the pine table and gestured towards Tom, standing beside the hearth. 'How is the brave lad, Mrs Perkins?'

'Well enough, milady.'

'I will have a surprise for our hero tonight, Mrs Perkins. And I have brought young Anne, whom he plucked from the pond. Perhaps they could go for a stroll? While we discuss the harvest supper arrangements.'

'Yes, milady. Now you be lookin' sharpish, Tom, and mind yerself.'

Tom was quick to meet Anne at the door and escape his grandmother's venom.

'Found out where the little girl is from, milady?' asked Mrs Perkins.

'No, she's a complete mystery,' said Lady Waddell. 'But no trouble. I shall keep her with me until her history is discovered.'

Anne walked behind her rescuer into the orchard, between sweet-smelling branches propped up with timbers, so that the heavy load of green pears would not break the boughs.

'Tom, how old are you?' she asked.

'Ten, and I'm almost a man. I'm going to work the farm with Grandpa Perkins. And I'm never going home no more.'

'How did you learn to swim? You can swim, can't you? You pulled me out.'

'By watching the fishes and the ducks, and even the old dog, he can paddle about in the river.'

'I can dog-paddle!'

'Sure you can. Ain't you just another of God's creatures?'

They were beside the pond now, and Tom said, in that round voice that sounded so familiar, 'Let's have a swim!' He had his boots off before Anne could protest.

She took off the buttoned boots Lady Waddell had provided, and the outer layer of the strange clothes she had been dressed in personally by that kind woman. If she went back into the pond, she could swim home again, or at least float back to the hospital, and wake up from this strange dream or place in which she was lost.

Tom dived under the water and stroked his way across the pond. 'Come!' he called.

Anne jumped in. She was not afraid. She was familiar with this pond already. The water had a soft, gentle touch to it. Her eyes did not sting, even when she opened them and watched the lengths of green ribbon weed moving in the current. She surfaced and imitated Tom's arm movements until she was over to the other side. For half an hour they practised. Anne floated, relaxed. She felt serene and confident, like a duckling floating behind a mother duck. But she was still definitely a duck in the wrong pond.

'Heavens!' cried Lady Waddell when she found them. 'A water nymph she is, to be sure!'

*

'Was your gran angry about the swim?' Anne asked Tom later, at the harvest supper.

He nodded. 'Gave me a taste of the switch. But no matter. I've had worse than that from Da.'

'I wish I was brave. I wish I was like you, Tom.'

'Like me?' Tom laughed, his brown eyes sparkling. 'But you are like me!'

He took her hand and dragged Anne merrily though the kitchen, down the dimly lit hall, into the heavily furnished front parlour. It was dark as they stood on the turkey rug beside the brass coal shuttle, except for the gleam of the fire in the cast-iron grate. Tom took a taper, and touched it to the small tongue of flame licking the burning coals. He lit two candlesticks on either end of the mantle. He stood Anne on a chair and bade her look in the gilt framed mirror high on the chimney breast.

'See, Chick?' said Tom, gazing at their reflection in the glass. 'Uncanny, ain't it? Like two peas in a pod, Gran says.'

Anne stared. Her straight, brown hair was familiar, but Tom's brown eyes and square, defiant chin were reflected not once, but twice. He was right. If not for the age difference, they might be identical twins.

'He is very, very like me from my heels up to my head,' she quoted.

Tom's puzzled face stared from the mirror.

'The poem!' explained Anne.

'Who are you, Anne?' asked Tom, soft as the candlelight. 'You didn't just fall from a pear tree into the pond! Why had you no proper clothes…?'

'I don't know. I mean, I shouldn't be here at all,' Anne said.

'Too right you shouldn't! What are you children playing at? Out of me best room this minute before I tan yer backsides. Hero or naught, Tom, you just mind yerself!' Gran shouted.

They went to join the crowd in the courtyard, sampling food laid out on a huge trestle lit by oil lamps. Lady Waddell made a speech and presented Tom with a book, in celebration of his heroic rescue of Anne from the pond. Anne hid in the kitchen, until Tom found her.

'Want a sip of perry?'

'A sip of what?'

'Perry. Don't you know nothin'? Cider comes from apples, and perry from pears. I stole a cup while Gran weren't looking. Here, try it.'

Anne sipped the strong fruity liquid; it was warm and velvety in her throat. She gulped more.

'Not too much!' cried Tom. 'It'll be hell to pay, if they find us worse for the perry.'

The room began a slow circle dance. Anne's feet were solidly placed on the stone flags of the kitchen, but everything, pine dresser, tinderbox, the large copper kettle on the hearth, was moving.

'Must – sit – a while,' Anne fumbled for the bench. She sat, but ended up lying, on the long oak seat.

Tom quickly drained the cup of any evidence. The room was spinning. Anne closed her eyes. Anne turned her head and spewed the contents of her stomach into an aluminum bowl.

*

'Caught that just in time,' said a cool, professional voice. Quick hands wiped her face with a damp cloth, took her pulse. A thin silver wrist watch gleamed in the narrow beam of a small torch.

'You'll do,' said the nurse. 'Although the anesthetic seems to have affected you more than most. Are you sure you didn't eat anything before the operation?'

Anne shook her head.

The white-soled shoes of the night sister trod softly away down the dim lit ward. Anne checked. It was a hospital bed she lay in – chrome bed frame, white sheets and a blue cotton bedspread woven with a crest. She reached into the drawer of the bedside chest, pushed aside her doll and grasped Tom's book. She leant back into the crisp hospital pillow, turned to her favorite page and read, 'I have a little shadow…'

The Patchwork Professor

He was a book collector: the walls of his study, all twelve foot high of them, were lined with higgledy-piggledy shelves of leather-bound, paperback, foolscap, quarto and pocket-sized editions of every book, journal and reprint he had ever read. He never threw out books or returned his borrowings from the libraries he frequented. He occasionally lent a tome to a friend, more often, borrowed one and never gave it back. The walls and floor and tables, of which there were many in this generous Victorian-built, vault-like study, were a patchwork of other people's dreams and visions. Like a collector of brain cells in a laboratory, he collected experiences of other people, lives of other times, journeys to other places. Beyond the walls of the university, his body rarely ventured – but his mind travelled far and wide, experiencing everything that was held between the bookbinder's sturdy covers. It was paradise.

The room was dim, lit only by desk lamps on tables dotted around the room. A chandelier suspended from the cavernous ceiling had once been run on gas, but had never been converted to electricity. Its crystals were grimy and dust-laden, home to spiders of unknown variety, who looped their traps from drop to drop, creating a fine lacework to entrap their prey. I do not know what they caught, on which species they feasted – but I am sure that bookworms never ventured to those heights, preferring the down-filled easy chairs below.

Neither did Casper, the professor's wily cat, who climbed bookshelves without fear and had secret sleeping places behind books and perches on shelves way above human eye level. He would emerge suddenly, with a spring, just when Adam had relaxed into one of the easy chairs with an article to read or a paper to revise. Adam was a graduate student, and a favourite of the professor, who liked Adam's bumbling reticence and the quick wit that just occasionally showed itself in their tutorials each Thursday afternoon. Adam was invited to make use of the professor's library, which he did, a lonely young man living alone pursuing his passion for history and having no need of pub crawls or football matches. If it weren't for Casper, Adam would have felt totally at ease in this musty cave of words.

The lamps in the room were a little younger than the long-extinguished chandelier, but still vintage. Their cloth-covered electric cords were frayed and twisted. When the professor wanted a book from an upper shelf, he took a battery-operated torch from a desk drawer and searched the gilt titles with a small steady halo of light. Failing that, if the torch had been mislaid or the batteries used up, there was always a match or lighter from the pouch where an ancient pipe and tobacco resided in the professor's pocket.

Adam puzzled over this, that the same man might use both matches and lighter, when usually habit dictated one or another. He put it down to eccentricity; and if the colour of the soft chamois pouch looked to be a different shade on different days, he put it down to the variable lighting; and if the timbre of the professor's voice sometimes was harsher, sometimes more mellow, he put it down to the combined effects of alcohol and tobacco.

Whether match or lighter, it would be held up dangerously high to light the way as the professor clambered on library steps, themselves littered with volumes too recent to gain a place on the stacks.

No one knows whether it was the fault of a frayed electric flex or an upheld flame that finally caused the empire of dry paper, cloth and card to burst into willing combustion. The professor perished in the blaze; the fire consumed many rows of books on the west wall and most of the room was ruined by soot and water damaged from the firefighters' hose. The building was saved by their efforts; but the professor and his library were no more.

The building was cordoned off for a week, while the proper investigations were carried out. When at last the barriers were taken away, the housekeeper and the college fellows began to sort through the debris.

Adam arrived, uninvited, appalled at the destruction. 'He lent me some of his books. Do you think it is all right to keep them?' he asked Dr John Bryant, a senior fellow, who was peering through the gloom, wondering if some of the top shelves might still hold salvageable tomes.

'Yes…I think he would like you to, lad,' replied the fellow.

Adam smiled in relief. 'And…and…'

'What is it, Adam?'

'One of them was the first…of a trilogy. Do you think…'

'Adam, my boy, if you can find the other volumes of a three-part work in this mess, you are welcome to them.' To his colleagues, Dr Bryant said, 'I don't think we can salvage anything at all in this sodden wreck. We'll list everything in the college insurance claim.'

'Nothing was catalogued,' mourned another.

'All irreplaceable, really,' said another.

'He never threw anything away,' replied Dr Bryant. 'All we have to do is make a list of all the references in his writing, and there we would have a complete list of his library.'

'But who would willingly undertake such a task?' he wondered aloud, shaking his head.

*

The following Thursday, Adam walked home alone after attending his morning classes, thinking of all the calm afternoons he'd spent in the professor's study, that now would be no more. Checking the mailbox on the way into his flat, he pulled out the weekly letter from his mother in Brighton, a few colourful flyers for real estate, and a slim white envelope with a solicitor's logo in the corner. He ripped it open and read the contents, turned away from the front door and jogged down the steps, back down the road to town.

'He's left me what?' exclaimed Adam, jumping up from the buttoned leather chair in the solicitor's office.

'His entire library, copyright of his published work, and all his office contents.'

'The mad old bugger.' Adam turned red from his neck to his ears and apologised to the silver-haired woman who was partner in the legal firm handling the professor's will.

'Yes, indeed,' she smiled. 'Quite literally. Which accounts for the lack of offspring, and any heirs to speak of.'

'Oh dear.'

'Yes, it will be a life's work sorting and reading and cataloguing.'

'Err…any money attached?'

'A small annuity. The professor was only rich in…shall we say…the written word.'

*

Adam was a diligent young man. He had seen his future, in some dim, unimagined kind of mist, working in academia, living in a university town, spending long hours with books and papers and ideas. The prospect of being his professor's posthumous secretary seemed daunting, but the more he thought about the reality, the more logical it seemed. His own research ideas were, after all, still largely unformed, and his potential doctoral thesis just a few multiplying cells of ideas, not even a fully developed foetus. He accepted the challenge and began work.

Although the soggiest, sootiest books of the west side of the professor's library had been cleared away, the floor roughly cleaned, and the area made safe, there was still a large area on the eastern side of books to be sorted and searched. He was still hoping to find the two further volumes of the trilogy.

The first of the trilogy was an odd book – a strange choice for a history professor to recommend. Melodramatic in tone, ponderous in language, it detailed the travels of a young rake in the eighteenth century. Despite himself, Adam was drawn in by the narrative. The naivety of the persona, and the wonder with which experiences were observed and recorded, entranced Adam beyond normal curiosity. It was the hunt for the next two volumes of the story that spurred him on in the sorting and sifting of the remnant library.

Although some cleaning had been done, there were still small piles of ashy debris, drenched and pulverised fragments of documents scattered over the scorched floorboards. The carpets had been removed, leaving a gritty surface over which Adam's feet crunched.

Coming into the room one Thursday, he saw small paw prints tracked over the corner of the room. 'Casper!' he called. He had forgotten about the professor's cat. Could Casper still be hiding somewhere in the ruined shelves?

Adam sought out the housekeeper and obtained some morsels of herring and a saucer of milk.

'I never thought the cat could have survived,' she wailed. 'I thought the poor thing perished with the professor.'

They left the food in the centre of the room, and waited quietly in the hall.

'I'll fetch you some tea,' said the housekeeper. 'Lord knows you have little enough home comforts in this burnt-out bombsite. Worse than the blitz!'

After a while, Casper not having appeared, Adam tiptoed into the room and began crating up some damp bundles of unbound papers that could be salvaged. The university archivists had advised to freeze the papers to stall the growth of mildew, until they had time to deal with the task of proper conservation. Adam had located an unused freezer in a nearby college. Carting the papers was a problem, but Dr Bryant had promised to arrange a vehicle. As Adam turned to begin on the next crate, he saw Casper chewing on the herring. Never on the best of terms with the cat, he waited until the feline had finished eating, then took small, gentle steps towards him. Casper, blackened around the tail and whiskers but otherwise in good shape, turned and fled into a corner. Adam bounced over boxes, determined not to let the cat evade capture. He used the professor's torch, flashing the beam to locate the cat on an upper shelf. Casper was in a deep alcove formed by a round porthole-shaped window set into the thick masonry wall. Unsurprisingly, the alcove itself was lined with books. Casper was reclining on one of these. Adam was astounded to see that it was the third volume of the trilogy he sought. The second was on the ledge of the stained-glass window. Deftly making a sling from his pullover, Adam rescued not only the cat but also his bed of precious reading. The cat did not resist. It was, after all, the pet of a gentleman scholar, not a feral animal.

Adam took the cat home to his own flat. He cleaned Casper with a damp towel. There seemed to be no serious injury to the cat. He fed him again and arranged a cosy spot for him by the radiator. Adam settled on the sofa with the second book of the trilogy and began to read.

The gothic script of the book wavered and danced before Adam's tired eyes. He dislodged the weighty book from its resting place on his chest and pushed it aside. He slept.

When he woke, Adam could still feel a weight on his chest, but opening his gritty eyes, he could see that it was not the book that weighed on him to the point of breathlessness, but Casper. Surprised, he put out his hand to scratch behind the cat's ear. Even more surprised, Adam heard the deep, throaty vibrations of the cat's purr.

It didn't take long to get into a new routine, of feeding Casper, securing him the flat for the day, attending a token lecture, spending the afternoon in the professor's library. Casper seemed happy in this new arrangement.

Adam sought permission to take temporary ownership of the unused dining hall in the college. He laboriously toted all the redeemable books and laid them on tables, and on the floor like dominoes. At last, the professor's library was emptied, and tradesmen moved in to rebuild the ash-grimed shell.

Adam's mother sent home-made cures for the cough Adam developed from the sooty residue. 'Always your weak point, your lungs,' she wrote. 'Better come down here for some good sea air.'

Adam replied that he couldn't leave the cat – and besides, he was making real headway with the bibliography of the professor's collection. Although there were years of work ahead of him to do a complete job, there was a pattern emerging. What puzzled Adam as he read and reread, listed and checked book chapters, journal articles and essays written by the professor, was how similar they were to others in the piles of reading he had catalogued. He checked and double checked. It was as if there were three distinct voices in the writing of the professor's publications. And these three voices were those of other academics in the university. At last, he realised that he could avoid the truth no longer.

The professor was a plagiarist.

None of his work was original; it had all been stolen from colleagues. The worst sin an academic could commit. Adam went home to his flat despondent, able to confide only in Casper. How could he besmirch the good name of the professor to whom he owed his livelihood, his *raison d'être*? He turned to reread the trilogy, which had so sunk into his consciousness that it was his daily comfort, rather like a warm bath to sink into at the end of the day. It was a tale of reincarnation, over and over, of the persona being reborn in places now lost in time. So many personalities, so many adventures, all with a single thread of narration. So many lives in one…

The doorbell rang.

Reluctantly, Adam pushed Casper off his knee and went to answer the door.

'Good evening, lad,' said Dr Bryant.

With the doctor were two other professors. In the evening dimness, Adam noted with innocent eyes how alike they seemed, in nondescript tweed jackets, hands thrust in pockets, grey hair receding in a typical male baldness pattern on each head. One pulled out a tobacco pouch and pipe. They trooped in and sat around the living room on whatever they could find, Casper taking the sofa.

'It's like this, lad,' began Dr Bryant, 'we know you must have worked it out by now. Our plan succeeded quite well for a long time.

But now…time to let you in on it. There was a vacant academic post at our disposal. None of us are rich men. We needed more income, so we faked a colleague. We created an identity, wrote his papers, secured his appointment and shared his income. We managed to stand in personally whenever required, which wasn't often. No one ever questioned it. But when you came along, it all got a bit risky. So we decided it was time to kill him off. The idea of him, I mean.'

'You mean there never was my professor? But…I met with him! There was a…a body!' protested Adam.

'You met with us. We even took turns…you were so shy, never making eye contact, you never even noticed.' Dr Bryant laughed. 'A homeless man had been living in the college garden gazebo for years,' said the professor, puffing a pipe. 'We just waited for him to pass – of natural causes I must add – then transferred him to the library. Set it alight. It went like the blazes.'

'But you left Casper?'

'No indeed…he snuck back in. And it seemed a good way to lead you to the second and third books.'

'But why?'

'We thought it would give you the clue you needed. That the professor was a patched-together persona, that his life was all a tale. But it seems you weren't quite up to it, lad.'

'Well …what do you expect me to do now?'

'Keep quiet, maintain the fiction, if you will. There's enough money to keep us all comfortable in retirement. We can help you gain a PhD, a decent appointment…perhaps in another regional university…or even overseas…'

Adam laughed. 'At a safe distance, you mean? You were him – and you – and you! The conversations we had…you know all about me!'

'You didn't reveal all that much. But we like you. We all liked you. Our patchwork professor liked you.'

Dr Bryant put out his hand and, after a long pause, Adam shook it. 'Thank…thank you, professor.'

Casper roused himself from the sofa and curled his tail around Adam's legs. The academics made their farewells and left. The cat leapt up on the bookshelves above the desk and stared at Adam with an unblinking gaze.

You were in on it too, thought Adam, as he reached up and stroked the cat's ear. He'd been duped, manipulated, played for a fool, even by this knowing feline. But he had also been handed a story idea unlike any other. A best-seller book, or evidence to be used against those devious old academics as blackmail? The choice was his. With Casper's purring loud in his ear, Adam went to his desk and began to write.

He was a book collector; the walls of his study, all twelve foot high of them, were lined with higgledy-piggledy shelves of leather-bound, paperback, foolscap, quarto and pocket-sized editions…

The Book Safe

'So sorry, it's water-damaged.' I tried to turn the customer away from the oak-balustraded staff area, back to the loaded bookshelves.

'No, really…it doesn't matter! I can't find that novel anywhere, it's not in the public library or the university… I've scoured all the other bookshops. I don't mind at all…can still read it, water damage or not.' She was adamant, persistent, pushy.

There is nothing, I have found, as self-important as a thwarted reader. 'It's against shop policy,' I lied, 'to sell anything in a substandard condition. And customers are definitely not allowed in the work area… rules about health and safety.'

She looked, greedily, through her rectangular crimson-framed glasses at the book clamped firmly in the bookbinder's press. The large gilt title was clearly visible, wedged in the hefty press, amongst a litter of linen binding thread, real-bristle brushes in jam jars, and pots of specialist glue. I have suggested to Dora, more than once, that a partition wall instead of the waist-height oak barrier might provide more privacy. But no, according to my boss, the old-fashioned book press and binding tools add an air of authenticity, even gravitas, to the shop atmosphere. The gold letters on the book spine mocked me with their recently cleaned brilliance: *One All Hallows Eve* by E.M. Finch.

Then came the inevitable phrase, delivered in a measured, unemotional but strong voice with just the hint of a smirk: 'I would like to speak with the manager.'

I was ready: oh yes, I have dealt with enough difficult people to know how the script goes. 'So sorry, the manager is away on a buying trip,' I intone with just the right practised pitch of regret, control and honeyed firmness.

Her frustration betrayed her by an infinitesimal twitch of the mouth, a toss of the well-groomed head. She handed me an embossed business card from the depths of her velvet patchwork tote. 'Hold that book for me. Have the manager call me the moment he returns.' She grasped a brochure from the stand beside the cash register. 'What was your name?' she enquired loudly, having just noticed the small wires curving into my ears.

'Rupert,' I lied. 'I'm the only Deaf employee here, so the boss will know who you're complaining about.'

She turned and retreated across our well-patinated, wide timber floorboards, which squeak loudly at just the right places to let you know when a customer is browsing the tall forest of bookshelves. I have no trouble at all picking up both the sound and the vibrations. If truth be told, a customer is at much more risk of injury between those heavily loaded stacks than in the work area, with its bench in front of the window looking over the sunny, cobbled laneway. Such a pleasant spot for a morning coffee.

I had been sipping just such a coffee yesterday morning, while unpacking a shipment of books. It was a slow weekday – not much passing trade and no bus tours expected. We are one antiquarian bookshop in a town of many bookshops: a concentration of similar establishments, popular with bus trips and booklovers, arts festival attendees and writers' workshops held in local venues. But it is the off-season, and the boss really is away buying books. I didn't tell that woman that I am the live-in lover of the boss as well as her right-hand man. She won't get any satisfaction from my darling Dora. I can see us chuckling over a bottle of lovely pinot noir one evening when Dora is home again, as I stroke her well-rounded hip in front of the wood fire. In the meantime, I am master of all I survey.

But it is still my job to unpack boxes, dust off books bought in job lots, and sort the trash from the saleable items. The box I unpacked yesterday morning was a mixed bunch: somebody's deceased estate. A miscellaneous collection of textbooks and novels, inspirational self-help works and poetry packed directly from shelf to cardboard carton. Birthday cards, shopping lists and the odd local newsletter were interleaved with the book pages. These items of serendipity could be much more interesting than the books themselves in a batch like this. I often find myself reconstructing the lives of previous book owners from the detritus they have left behind in their reading matter. There might be a spare passport photo used as a bookmark: which lends the imaginative exercise an undeserved flavour of integrity. It was such a morning yesterday, customerless and leisurely, and I drank a full pot of good coffee while sifting through the musty piles.

There were a few good, classic novels we could sell; a vintage street directory a local artist would be interested in for collage; the poetry was mostly unknown to me. I put those slim tomes aside for Dora to look at. There was a chunky hardback, battered and insect-eaten down the edges. It didn't look worth saving. I checked all the other items for signs of infestation, but they were clean. Nothing worse for a bookshop than introducing mould or pests. Paper, for all its usefulness, is a vulnerable material. It burns easily, water ruins it, insects love to feast on it. Paper tears, creases and browns with age. So like a human body: maybe that is why we love our books as we do.

The damaged novel looked like the sort of epic I had enjoyed as a teenager. Black and white maps on the endpapers, lists of characters, family trees and many, many chapters. Just the thing to while away the night hours in Dora's absence. I opened it and flipped through…an irregular, vermin-eaten hole lay right smack in the middle of the volume. I tossed it into the bin.

I closed the store and walked to the pub. With Dora away, I'd have a snack meal this evening. A hot lunch appealed.

Dora is the world to me. Ever since that first day I wandered into her bookshop, and saw the 'Help Wanted' sign, she's been my everything. After my arts degree, I had searched for work, but everything always led to teaching, and who could face explaining, year after year, to each new group of noisy children in each new class, about hearing impairment and my cochlear implants? Amuse them with the rudiments of British Sign Language (BSL) and then do it all again the next year? No thanks. A library studies diploma gave me various skills. But libraries are closing down all over Britain: hard enough for employed librarians to keep their jobs, let alone start a new career. Which left me in Lower Woerking-on-Tyne, browsing Dora's shop. When she signed 'hello' in BSL it was a lifeline thrown out to a drowning sailor.

Yes, Dora is my world. But how nice sometimes, to walk down the street with money in your pocket, go into the pub and buy a counter lunch? Shout the men conversing there a round and enjoy their company? I did enjoy it. But after an hour, cheered by the ale, I went back to work.

I cleaned and priced those saleable recent arrivals, added them to the stock list. I dusted (yes, dusted) the front counter, adjusted the brochures and bookmarks. I chose some enticing art books and changed the window display to surprise Dora. A painting course was scheduled at the local arts centre – might pull in some passing trade. Then I made tea and sat at the work bench to sort out the mending pile. I did a bit of judicious excising of blank pages scribbled on with green wax crayon at the end of a classic edition of *Winnie the Pooh*. It'd sell on the specials table. I reglued a cover on a dictionary and sewed up a loose Shakespeare with linen thread. I'm quite good at this. Dora is pleased with me – she hasn't the patience for repairs.

The bell over the shop door tinkled; the small warning light flashed above my worktable.

It was Bob, from the arts centre, who I had seen earlier in the pub. 'I've something you'll appreciate, Davey,' he whispered. 'The missus being away, and all that.' He pulled out a bag of pot. 'Best grade, special price, just for you.'

Bob, crafty devil, knew I was in charge of the till that day. But I didn't take the necessary cash from the drawer. I took out my own wallet and paid the man. That the money was a bit extra I'd been saving to surprise Dora at Christmas, was neither here nor there. Something would turn up.

Looking around for a safe place to put the weed, my eyes landed on the book in the wastebasket. I retrieved it, picked up my sharp blade and began enlarging the cavity in the middle of the book. One ear cocked for the sound of the bell, one eye on the warning light, I worked steadily through the afternoon. It was satisfying work, carving words from an overstuffed novel full of its own importance. Or so it seemed, as I tried out one of Bob's joints. When the hollow was complete, I took a brush and glue, began sticking together the rim of pages. It was long after official closing time when I finished, clamped the book holding the remaining weed into the book press, and wound the screws tight. I did not know it would cause me such grief the next day.

*

'There is a letter,' said Dora a week later, 'from a Dr Eunice Partridge. Who says she is researching E.M. Finch, and that you refused to sell her the last remaining copy in England of that author's book, *One All Hallows Eve*. What say you?'

I signed something very rude behind Dora's back.

'I saw that!' she exclaimed, looking at my reflection in the shop window. 'You forget my father was deaf.'

Bless his soul, that deaf father is probably the reason Dora takes so much interest in me. I thank my lucky stars for him every day.

'I'm sorry. I love you,' I signed. I hugged her from behind, kissed her neck.

She read on. 'Your shop assistant, going by the name of Rupert...' and here she giggled, because I had been musing over a second-hand copy of *Rupert Bear* that first day in her shop, and it is her pet name for me, 'Rupert insisted that the book is water-damaged and unable to be sold. May I offer to pay double the recommended retail price (which I have ascertained from Amazon even though there is no stock with that supplier)...' and here Dora herself swore, because she abhors Amazon above all else, 'for that damaged copy which is the only one I have been able to locate. I am unable to finish my research on E.M. Finch (a student and friend of Tolkien) without this text. Yours sincerely,...'

'So where is it? 'asked Dora. 'Where is this damnable book?'

'I threw it out.'

'Threw it out? When she asked you to hold it?'

'I didn't know she seriously needed it. It didn't look special. There must be some others around.'

'Libraries have weeded their collections to death, collectors concentrate on antiquities…less popular authors just haven't been archived.'

'I thought she would just go away. You know. People say they will return but never do. I had the book in the press, I was trying to save it, but it was insect-infested, foxed, damp and mouldy…it smelt. So I threw it away.'

'The shop isn't doing so well, you know,' Dora said.

'I'm sorry. I make mistakes…you shouldn't leave me in charge.'

'No sense in crying over spilt milk,' said Dora gently. 'Is that the time? I'm meant to be at the auction. Open the shop for me, love.'

'Sure,' I replied. But first, I took my improvised book safe, with its illegal contents, from the drawer where I had hidden it. I wrapped it in a dust jacket borrowed from a similar-sized book. It fitted well. I stowed the book in the middle of the mending pile.

To ease my conscience, I took out a pile of catalogues from other booksellers, and trawled their lists for another copy of *One All Hallows Eve*. It was a thankless task.

Dora returned and sat at her desk to deal with her special orders. 'I was sure this first edition had a dust jacket,' said Dora. 'Did you see it? The buyer only wants it if complete with original cover.'

'I took it off to remove some old sticky tape,' I improvised. 'Give it here, I can find the cover.'

Some tourists came in. Dora chatted about village landmarks and sold the women some postcards; showed the men some maps and books on local history. I whisked out the dustjacket and replaced it on the first edition. I wrapped my secret book safe in brown paper, addressed it to myself. Don't ask me why. Perhaps a memory of some B-grade crime film. I really don't know.

'Just going out to the post office,' I called.

It was good to walk around. I was relieved to have the weed out from under Dora's nose. She would freak if she found it. I wouldn't upset darling Dora for all the world.

'There you are, Rupert Bear,' she smiled as I entered the shop. 'I'm making cocoa. Want some?'

Fortified with hot cocoa I checked Amazon (Dr P was right, no stock and a hideous recommended retail price), the Book Depository, every supplier in the business. Everywhere, I drew a blank. There had only been one small print run of this novel. J.R.R. Tolkien himself had written the introduction. I could see why Dr P had been desperate.

At last, at long, long last, a second-hand bookseller's website showed two available copies. I jumped out of my seat in excitement and grabbed Dora's credit card, purchased both copies, with express shipping. One copy was in New Zealand, another in California. I breathed a sigh of relief.

*

A deluge of orders came in before Christmas. My table was covered with piles of work. Short of cash, having wasted money on that dope, I worried how to buy something nice for Dora. She decorated the shop in Dickensian style, with frosted windowpanes and holly around the shelves. She sent out invitations to partake in mince pies and mulled wine on Christmas Eve. Dora does nothing by halves.

My dad rang: my sister and her brood were coming for Christmas. Dora and I prefer a quiet visit with just my parents – a mixture of BSL, spoken word, and laughter. My parents had seen me devotedly through the challenges of childhood: were relieved, if surprised, to see me settle down with an older woman.

'We are much too busy,' I replied. 'But would love to come in the New Year.'

'See you then, son,' replied Dad. 'Mum sends love, and says there's something in the post.

On Christmas Eve, I was sorting through a deluge of mail, while Dora warmed her spicy brew. In one package, I found a woollen scarf knitted by my mother, and a card with two hundred pounds taped inside. In another, the New Zealand copy of *One All Hallows Eve*.

'Eureka!' I shouted. 'Call Dr Partridge in a pear tree. Her book arrived.'

'Parcel it up,' directed Dora. 'And race down to the post office.' She went to adjust the fairy lights strung around the outside tables.

I opened another parcel: it was the book I had posted to myself, containing illegal contents. I compared it with the book from NZ. Identical. A customer came in wanting *A Christmas Carol*. He spent ages comparing the three available copies in the shop. I sweetened him with some of Dora's mulled wine: he bought the most expensive copy. Pleased with myself, I went back to my table, opened another package. The Californian book had also arrived.

I invoiced Dr Partridge for the cost of both books plus a mark-up and shipping costs. Enclosing our shop Christmas card, I wrapped up the books, wound my new scarf around my neck, and jogged to the post office, kissing Dora on the cheek as I passed.

I went to the jeweller and bought the antique diamond pin Dora had been eyeing for months. I bought champagne and chocolate truffles, took them home and put them all under our small Christmas tree.

We closed the shop late on Christmas Eve. The mince pies were all eaten and the mulled wine enjoyed. We put up the closed sign and went home to our cosy flat to hibernate. It snowed: for the first time ever, I surprised Dora with a decent present. We didn't reopen the shop until after going to Devon.

I had forgotten all about my stash of weed. Back at my worktable I looked for the book safe in vain. It was nowhere to be seen.

'Oh…' said Dora as she cleared away a piece of forgotten mistletoe, 'that book for Dr Partridge, that extra one on your table. It looked a bit ratty, but I sent it off to her with the option to keep or return.'

'…what?'

'I sent off the extra copy.'

'But why?'

'Not likely to sell it to anyone else.'

I waited for the inevitable letter to arrive. I snaffled it from the mail-bag as soon as I saw the envelope bearing Dr Partridge's name. It read,

Dear Rupert and Dora

Thank you for the copies of *One All Hallows Eve* by E.M. Finch which came by recent post. Please find herein a cheque for the invoiced amount.

I appreciate the extra effort you have made to secure these books for me.

The enclosure was especially enjoyable: did all your customers receive this special holiday treat?

With thanks,

Dr Eunice Partridge.

'What does she mean?' asked Dora.

'…the Christmas card?'

'Strange way to put it.'

'Does it matter? Look at the size of the cheque!' I kissed Dora and made a cheeky suggestion in sign. Her reply was totally satisfactory.

Blood and Deceit

I am a crime writer. I am a crime writer sick and tired of it…worn down by the blood and deceit, the conniving and trickery in my books. As each manuscript reaches the publisher, I think, *That's it, that's the last.* But Gus won't let me alone.

Augustus Crabbe – not his real name, a self-styled detective, a third generation Hercule Poirot – keeps feeding me, hounding me with material. Crimes so heinous and irresistible in their ingenuity and design, their wit and brilliance, I can't turn away but must tap, tap, tap at the keyboard in a writing frenzy so as not to miss any of the vital details or nuances important to the reader's hold on the narrative thread.

He sends information by email. By fax if I avoid the computer for days on end. He sends newspaper clippings and police photographs by post. I try to ignore the bulky post bags but cannot last more than a day without ripping into the package, pouring myself a fortifying Scotch and laying out the contents on the living room floor, piecing together the gruesome jigsaw puzzle he has sent to keep me in his thrall.

More than once, I have gathered up the fragments in a rage at the enormity of the evil perpetrated on this earth, and moved to throw them into the open fire, but the novelist within can't bear to waste the material, vital and original in its authentic horror, and I begin once again to tell the story of the victim, the villain and the discovering detective. This is what the pay-off must be for Augustus, the hero, the avenging angel, the cleverer-than-thou opponent of the criminal. And the readers share this thrill.

It has been profitable. The thatched cottage within easy commute to London; the shiny motor in the drive; the annual trip to Barbados… but it is a lonely life, without my wife who packed up our daughters fifteen years ago and left in desperation, having been shut away from my life and work, and the festering evil lurking in the piles of note-books, photographs and envelopes in my study. I lock it all away, in many filing cabinets, and hide the keys.

So we go on together, Gus and I, in our collaboration, describing a litany of crimes, man's inhumanity to man. And to woman, and to child, to beast and to international corporation. He will drop by and sit in the twilight smoking with me, tossing around motive, alibis and the reliability of witnesses. Why am I the mouse in his trap? He once read and liked an article of mine in *The Examiner*, so he chose me to be his vehicle – wanting the world to know of his work and the evil that most of us are oblivious to in our daily round of eating, shopping, work-ing and loving.

I have tried to stop him sending the stuff…but he is resolute. I try to contact him with stern messages requesting no more material be sent, but he is untraceable, uncontactable. He supplies no phone number. If I reply to his email, it comes back 'undeliverable'. Postmarks on pack-ages are indecipherable, faxes come from untraceable numbers.

'What if I need you?' I ask.

'Never mind, old chap,' he replies mildly. 'I'll always find you.'

Mrs Henderson comes in daily to 'see' to me. She cooks a casserole, prepares lunch, washes and tidies. Loopy, the basset hound whose bas-ket lies empty beside the kitchen door, decamped to the neighbours when I went on a month's holiday and never came home. In a kind of ironic recompense, their black and white cat adopted me, and she sits on the wide windowsill in the sun where my wife's porcelain animals once stood in a row – watching out the diamond-paned casement win-dow or, if the weather is bad, she curls in front of my fire.

Occasionally, a photograph arrives from Australia showing slim, tanned young women, nothing like the downy-haired, dimple-chinned babies I remember… I suppose they gain some pleasure from name-dropping, their father the crime writer whose novels are adapted by the BBC and shown, in English and in subtitles, all over the world. But they aren't interested in seeing me. I'm the source of monetary support tucked away in the curiosity cupboard with the thatched cottages and field mice of their storybooks. And it is better that way.

So I go on – putting together evidence and narrative and explaining the criminal mind. And the public is fascinated, paying good money for the sanitised version of the evil that the publishers will allow. I can't give the full revolting horror Gus provides to me. The censor has come a long way but there are still limits to what the public stomach can handle.

Today, overwhelmed by the sheer pointlessness of the evil, I turn away from the computer, lock the front door and head across the fields breathing in the revitalising, cleansing, fresh country air.

Rambling down the shady laneway, green with overgrown hedges and wild violets, I turn away from the sign pointing to the village and climb the hill, where a rocky outcrop on the summit is warmed by the sun. But today, who should be there ahead of me, relaxed and at ease in his tweed jacket and cap, smoking a familiar pipe, but Augustus Crabbe.

'The evening called you out, too, old man?' he asks. 'I've got a picnic here if you want a bite.'

Beside Crabbe is a hamper with thermos, sandwiches, fruit. Sighing, I take a red apple and a knife and begin to peel the fruit.

'Dreadful business, this last case, don't you think?' he asks. 'Anything involving a child upsets me, but a whole family…truly diabolical, wouldn't you say? I've brought photos and the coroner's report for you.' He indicates a brown envelope protruding from the hamper.

My respite hijacked in this detestable manner, I am ruthless with the apple and plunge the blade into the juicy core, flicking out the seeds. The knife is sharper than I thought and I nick my thumb in the process. I suck the wound to staunch the blood.

'Lucky to have come across you like this, old chap. I was coming to see you after my picnic, of course. But now we can ramble down together, get a pint or two at the pub and end up at your place, can't we?

I've so much to tell you about the case. This one really eluded me till the last. I really thought it was the brother who...'

Maybe it was the sight of blood on my thumb or the sudden rush of the empowerment of a knife in my hand but as Augustus turned to survey the sun setting on the distant hills, I lifted the serrated blade and plunged it with all my might through the tweed between his shoulder blades. I gave it an extra thrust as his groan of surprise reached my ears. I did not care to see his wretched face but pushed him face down on the rocky outcrop. He was motionless. I could see his blood seeping onto the ground, darkening the pebbly grit and the moss. I had the presence of mind to wipe the knife handle, still in situ, with a napkin from the basket. I had touched nothing else, except the apple that I had eaten. The peel and the seeds lay around the feet of Augustus together with his sandwich crumbs. There was no hound to follow me home, no farmer watching in these deserted fields.

I went home and took Mrs Henderson's casserole from the freezer. There were no messages on the answering machine, no faxes. I cleaned my shoes thoroughly, top and bottom, and placed them in my suitcase. I added a lightweight suit, shirts, underwear, and my shaving kit. I poured a Scotch and soda, wrote a note to Mrs Henderson, logged onto my computer and booked a first-class ticket to Australia. Then, one by one, I deleted all the emails ever received from Augustus Crabbe.

The Artist's Eye

Absence. This park bench is about absence. This park bench is in the grounds of the artists' studio complex where Samantha has a borrowed space.

This park bench is empty. The grounds are deserted. Few people visit this converted institution during the week. It is ghostly, eerie, it has a haunted quality. It is late winter – there are still some brown leaves kicking around the bases of the bare elms. Shadows move and twist on the mock gothic landscape. Pigeons and rats are the only inhabitants of the arches and turrets of the nineteenth century terraced gardens and gabled outbuildings.

No one sits on the wooden planks of this seat. There are cigarette butts around the base of the bench, in amongst the brown leaf litter and torn grass, recently shredded by a tractor-driven lawnmower.

There is a high stone terrace, with a lethal drop to the stony, under-fed, under-filled river below, where a weir is coloured lime green with moss and the barest trickle of water can be heard between bird calls. Between the grimy glass of a disused greenhouse and an ancient clipped hedge, a magpie caught in a cage set for feral cats loses hope and expires.

*

The head curator stood, watching the gallery assistants unpack and hang the portrait, arms folded, chin in hand. A tall, lean man, Ken's limbs folded and unfolded slowly, deliberately, like a praying mantis. He rocked back and forth on his heels; eyes fixed on the gilt-framed rectangle of canvas now in place on the well-lit ivory wall. He stretched on his own white gloves over patrician fingers and adjusted the painting by a millimetre. Handing the spirit level back to the assistant, he sighed. The identifying plaque, in clearly accessible Arial font, was already adhered to the wall:

Portrait of a young girl
Artist unknown
circa 1870

The curator stroked his chin cleft with a cotton finger. He'd been criticised for accepting this painting. 'Pure chocolate box!' said his wife, Arlene Horst, the eminent art historian. They publicly claimed to never talk shop at home. Certainly, the child was very pretty. Luminous ringlets, buttery skin, lips heightened by ruby tones, jewel colours in swaths of drapery. It was in the mode of Renoir, French in rendering and design, but completely lacking in provenance. The donor was the spinster daughter of a veteran, whose father was said to have brought home the painting as a spoil of war.

Ken stepped back and recrossed his arms. He might just have hung a blatant fake or a stolen original. He traced, with a practised eye, the painterly brushstrokes of the child's plump fingers and smiled. A remembrance of his own daughter's sweetness, before Samantha became so angular and pierced, black and spiky. Let the critics sneer – chief among them, his wife – this one corner of the gallery would be his tribute to childhood. Had the gallery been empty, he would have leant forward and kissed those red child lips. He didn't. He went to his desk to puzzle over the documents of the donation, sip whisky and wonder what to put on the gallery insurance policy.

*

Samantha lent against the rough, rendered wall of the old hospital and lit a cigarette. She kicked the mondo grass edging the concrete pavers that sat oddly with the tessellated tiles of the turn-of-the-century veranda. What a mishmash of styles this place was! If it were up to her, she'd raze the lot to the ground and build a wide, open, glazed structure with a black, slanted roof like giant eagle wings ready to take flight. She hesitated to enter the building, to walk through the dreary corridors of institutional grey. Ash was piling up on the cigarette she held between her bare, anxious fingers. She flicked it towards the mondo grass. She only smoked occasionally, from boredom, in the way that her father sucked the whisky bottle, at home and in his office at the gallery. To fill in the time, to avoid binging on carbohydrates, to avoid thinking about the next thing, the next day, the next canvas. Her mouth felt foul and the cigarette, worse. She spat out the fag and squashed it with the sturdy heel of her black leather boot.

She didn't like this empty place, but it was convenient and spartan, with nothing to distract her from work in progress and no nagging doubts about whether her father had eaten a meal or whether her mother was due home from overseas or not. Away from home, she could put these worries about her parents into proper perspective. They were her parents, not her problem. She would worry about them later. She checked her watch and saw that it was already four p.m. The day was getting colder and she wanted to do three hours work at least. Her father thought she was out with friends, had learnt not to ask questions. She checked her phone: no messages. Mum usually sent a text once a day; she was off schedule. Samantha needed to talk to her, but in person, about doctors and appointments, about practical things and whether a baby could fit within their household. She was long past the time for abortion, although nothing really showed: Dad hadn't noticed a thing and Mum had been travelling for months.

Samantha's car was the only one in the car park. There was nobody else in the studios, apparently. Well, fine, no distractions then. She had work to do, in private, and this was the place to do it.

The hall she entered was hung with a temporary exhibition of student photographs of the usual things: black and white studies of homeless people, close-ups of unshaven old men on park benches, urban streetscapes. Beyond it, the old wards, large enough to be useful studio spaces, complete with running water, enhanced by new skylights, were completely functional; but no money had been spent to improve the corridors that connected the spaces, and the institutional feel of the building was intact, from the pitted mosaic mural in the atrium to the steel bars across the arched windows, the battered balustrades in the stairwell. Rolf's studio was on the first floor. Samantha's footsteps echoed on the stairs, like a pacemaker trying to pulse a dying body into life.

*

Trans-seasonal travelling is the pits. You planned to be practical and take matching, coordinated pieces, designed to be layered as required. But, afraid of the cold (and how dispiriting to be away from home, and cold in your very bones), Arlene always packed too many extra garments, thick socks and even a fluffy dressing gown, for who could feel really comforted by a thin, synthetic hotel blanket?

Her suitcase was a tumble of half-worn clothes and clean underwear – she hated that; usually kept neat, orderly piles even when travelling. But this morning she searched in haste for the silk shirt she knew she had packed, must have packed – but it was nowhere. Putting on a different, heavier knit top, she felt hot and hassled and out of sync. Arlene couldn't be bothered to sort out the tangle in her suitcase. Thought about ringing home, but knew there would be no answer. Thought about the life she had been living, the life she had wanted, and knew there was no synchronicity in any of it. She wondered how many bottles of whisky had been drunk in her husband's study this week. More, or less, in her absence? Why was there no clearer clue to his missing her, or wanting her there, not here? She opened her laptop, checked her schedule and decided to cancel the last appointment and fly home tomorrow. A few phone calls organised it, left no one feeling slighted. There was no point calling Ken. He owned a mobile phone but never remembered to turn it on.

Arlene remembered when untasted, still-wrapped airline food was a take-home surprise to be tucked into her carry-all for her daughter. She remembered the baby days, the soft pressure of new warm skin on her cheek – how she had willingly drowned in it, floated in it like bathwater, swum in it like an ocean pool. A touch so soft and gentle, enriching her, enlivening her, drenching her with spring rain. As a child Samantha had been tactile, loving, demonstrative, anxious not to be separated. She recalled how the down on the Sam's baby arm had tickled her neck each night as the child clung on for one last good night kiss. There was peace in these memories, and comfort of the most spiritual kind. Innocence. Nothing that could be saved or preserved. A jar of golden sherbet drops to be taken out and swallowed, one by one, until childhood was gone.

How long ago that all seemed. What would please her now? Clothes and jewellery she always got wrong. The only jewellery Samantha ever wore was a tiny silver cross, a christening gift from her grandmother. Some foreign art magazines, filled with glossy photographs of new work, were already tucked in her bag. On impulse she had also bought, from a stall in a backstreet market, a fat baby-faced buddha with a lopsided smile. She held the pendant in her hand, then touched the warmed green stone to her dry cheek. She had whisky in a duty-free bag for Ken. Arlene hadn't sent her daily text to Samantha, but would be home tomorrow, have a proper catch-up. She hoped her early return would be a welcome surprise.

She tipped out the mess that was her suitcase and began folding, sorting, repacking. There in the bottom of the suitcase was her silk shirt. Calm and smooth, unhassled and unworn. The cream folds were delicious to her fingertips.

*

Samantha's friends had warned that there might be an expectation of sexual payback for her use of Rolf's studio; but Sam knew she was just part of the general strategy to make it appear he was using the place, not ignoring the conditions of the grant. Rolf was strangely asexual, seeking out neither men nor women. He was focused on himself in a form of childish, unquestionable egocentrism.

An art school acquaintance, Rolf had the studio as part of an emerging-artist-in-residence programme, but hardly used it in winter, preferring to be at home, sketching as he lay under his doona, with a beanie and football socks layered on to keep out the cold. He went to the studio once a week, making sure he was noticed by the gardener, the volunteers, whoever was around to witness his occupancy. He phoned the administration to complain about the leak in the corner of his studio. He ordered pizza and gave inadequate directions, so the delivery boy had no choice but to knock on every studio door. Rolf could have been a public servant in another reincarnation. He had the arts bureaucracy eating marble chips out of his hand. He would emerge from his bedroom in the spring with a dozen or so carefully drafted charcoal drawings and convert them to large-scale canvases in a blaze of activity – there would be paint splashed energetically on the floor and sections of each painting worked on in a simultaneous frenzy of brushwork. The series that resulted would be thematically coherent and fully integrated into the philosophical bullshit he had been blogging onto his website all through the winter. He would need extra time in the studio to finish the collection – but when it was all over, the board would offer him a solo exhibition and free publicity. A mentoring role to next year's new artists. Rolf knew exactly how to work the system.

Samantha unlocked the steel door of the borrowed studio, locked the door on the inside and pocketed the key. She threw down her bag and took off the baggy jacket she had been wearing all winter. Rolf had enough sense to keep an efficient heater in the studio. She turned it on, rubbed her hands together in the warm air expelled from the whirring fan. She began pacing around the canvas that her father knew nothing about. Unlike her usual work, it was figurative, detailed, and lightly washed in the hues of ancient stained glass. Six foot by four, it was nothing she could keep secret at home.

She switched on the CD player, programmed to repeat Thais's 'Meditation', and began work.

*

Samantha sees the park bench from the high arched windows of the studio but doesn't focus on it. She sees shadows, the movement of light and the tracery of branches on the bare plaster wall. If she had looked, she might have seen the shape of a man, a man in a brown woollen coat, resting there a minute or two, before shuffling off, his feet silent on the soft, uneven ground.

She might have seen him, or she might not: the rich blue wash of the woman's cape was almost right; the red gleam of her jewelled bodice pleased her at last.

Sparrows flew in after the man had stepped away. Finding no crumbs, they didn't linger.

At last, Samantha pulled off her boots and stood flexing her toes, surveying her progress. The painting would take another day, possibly two. Her forearms ached and her brain was dulled from concentration. The background was still to be finished. The figures were done, she thought, but could not be sure. She needed to rest, could not continue without a break. She gathered her brushes and turned off the CD player.

She stirred the warm dozy liquid with her index finger, creating a spiral in the sludge below. It was heavy, this water, heavy with detergent and pigment. She stirred and whirled her hand to create a whirlpool of the sluggish purple pond in the stainless-steel trough. Cleaning brushes could take forever, and Rolf had left his soaking too, but she had no reason to go home.

Outside on the park bench, the man in the brown woollen coat had reappeared, but she didn't notice him.

Sam thought about sleeping the night in the studio. There was a clean enough sleeping roll in the corner of the room – another of Rolf's gestures to his make-believe work ethic. There was a large can of veg-etable soup on the paint-splattered ledge above the sink, a tin of crack-ers, and a microwave in the common kitchen area down the hall. Instant coffee, but no milk. A sleep, an early start at first light, and she might be finished tomorrow. She dried her hands, took the can of soup and padded to the kitchen, her green woollen socks catching on the splin-tered floor of the hallway.

She was reading the tiny microwave directions on the label when the man in the brown woollen coat grabbed her from behind.

*

It was her shadow self who walked alone along the leaf-blown path to the weir, and contemplated the moss on the cobbled creek bed. She climbed down and lay on the wet pebbles, allowing the brackish water to trickle into the dry folds of her clothes, her skin.

In the secret places of her body, another life slowly pulsed to silence. It took longer, but was just as quiet in the change from being to non-being. The little shadow rose in the wind and caressed her mother shadow as they evaporated into the rising mist.

Dead. As dead as the empty cigarette lighter Rolf pulled out of the pocket of his brown woollen coat and tossed into the murky river. He walked purposefully up the bank to the studio. Time to stir up some paint.

*

She was dead, as dead as the wreath of flowers that had been delivered, fresh, to the house two weeks ago on the day of the funeral. Arlene had enjoyed the fragrance of the freesias, stooped to consider the pale lemon markings on the open throats of these spring flowers, white in their purity, audacious in their scent, temporary in their existence. And recoiled in sudden guilt at her enjoyment of the flowers, when her daughter, her sweet absent child, was now a pile of ash waiting to be collected from the crematorium.

Brown and withered the flowers fell, dropping pollen on the ebony table in the hall. The house was layered with a film of dust. There were used dishes, newspapers, clothes strewn in the most unlikely places. The housekeeper, superstitious and full of grief, had quit on the day of the funeral. She wouldn't work in a house of death, Marie said, even with her heavy gold cross prominently displayed on her bosom. Had listened in on the phone call that revealed to Samantha's parents that her murder

160

had robbed them not only of their daughter, but their grandchild as well. That girl had always been up to no good, thought Marie.

Ken and Arlene's mourning was unorderly and conspicuous. Neither of them had left the house. Visitors were turned away, email was unread. The phone was never answered, and the machine had reached the limit of stored messages. The door of their home studio, full of Samantha's bold acrylics and mixed media constructions, had not been opened.

Rolf came, with a mate in a borrowed van. The six-by-four canvas was wrapped neatly in brown paper, sealed with masking tape. He shook Ken's hand and clasped his shoulder, explained about the painting. Left it propped up in the hall beside the flower-strewn table.

When Rolf was gone, Samantha's parents tore at the wrapping like feral cats and stood, speechless, at the calm beauty of the revealed figures. A king and queen, in regal robes of medieval design, stood hand in bejewelled hand, gazing with mournful purpose from the flat surface of the canvas. This final painting was unlike anything their daughter had ever produced before. Richly coloured, translucent, lit from behind as if it were a stained-glass window. To see their own emerald and sapphire eyes, transmuted into these almond-shaped gems located in the elongated, Modigliani-shaped faces, that were nevertheless their own, was an assault on both their hearts and their minds.

It was if they saw each other through their daughter's eyes. Through a mirror of her own invention, a kind of reverse *Portrait of Dorian Grey*.

Ken stepped across the tiled floor of the foyer where they still stood, and ran a shaking hand over the surface of the painting. It was as tall as he, and he had never stretched a canvas as large as this for his daughter's use. Should he have? Should he have asked what she needed? Why did she hide this from them, why, oh WHY had she been in that damn borrowed studio at all?

He looked at the background more carefully, and felt with clumsy fingertips the rough patches of primer still showing through, could understand the parts Samantha had not finished. He knew how she would have stippled this stone colour around the figures and darkened the shadow below the angled sill, that was still merely etched out in pale charcoal. He knew that the gothic windowpanes would have been finished with a blaze of pure light. He knew that there would have been a final touch of high illumination on the chalice that gleamed aloft in the right hand of the queen.

He turned and saw his wife, and saw that she was every bit as majestic as the woman in the painting, although convulsed in silent tears.

*

At the gallery, the curator inspects a newly hung exhibition by the artist Rolf McKann, one-time friend of his lost daughter. How sympathetic Rolf had been after her death! With his boyfriend, he had visited Ken and Arlene and drawn them back into daily life. As they grew closer, it was only natural that Ken should help Rolf get established in his career. In one of the paintings, the cut-off view of a woman's throat shows a small silver cross against the beautiful line of her collarbone. Something buzzes in the curator's head; he rubs his wrinkled temple. Walks away to find a coffee. He has given up whisky, has not replaced the bottle that once lived in his filing cabinet.

From the gallery café, he observes the grey outline of the city against the rain-laden skies. Bracts of flowering eucalypt, like cheerleader pom-poms, wave at him as if signalling a message. The air currents strengthen and the city lights begin to come on. Arlene will be here soon. They have begun eating dinner together, companionably, in restaurants, prolonging the hours before they must go home. They will take a trip overseas soon, and both intend to take a long absence from work. A cottage in Kent has been offered them for the English summer, and they will gladly accept the change.

As they drive through the city, diagonal ripples of rainwater in the gutter, cross-hatched by the lines left by the concreter's trowel, bother him with an irrational sense of déjà vu. Arlene drives, as she has done ever since Sam's death. Ken should get his eyes checked for new glasses, but doesn't want to know. Caught in a snarl of traffic, they sit in silence and wait for the outward lanes to clear. Ken turns the radio on and the tones of Thais's 'Meditation' fill the car. He struggles to focus on the cars beyond the rain-streaked windscreen. He observes that Arlene is moved by the music. The banked-up car brake lights gleam red, staring back at him, like a host of devil eyes.

Acknowledgements

'Movement' first published online *Verity La* 2011, republished *The Hunger* (ebook anthology, best of Verity LA) edited by Michele Seminara, Robbie Coburn & Nigel Featherstone, Verity La, 2018.

'Waiting' first published *The Hungry Chimera,* Issue 3, October 1, 2017

'In Good Company' HC Adrien Abbot Prize 2013 first published online https://jthorndyke.wordpress.com/stories/

'The Cave' Phoenix 2007 (USYD Writers' Journal); republished online in *The Moon Magazine* http://moonmagazine.org/julie-anne-thorndyke-the-cave-2017-04-29/

'Blood and Deceit' first published *Mystery Weekly* 2016

'On the Bus' first published online *Ancient Paths* 28 April 2018

'Your Middle Name' first published 3 June 2016 *Flash Fiction Magazine* http://flashfictionmagazine.com/blog/2016/06/03/your-middle-name/

'The Artist's Eye' FAW Pauline Walsh Short Story First Prize 2011; published online https://jthorndyke.wordpress.com/stories/

'Houseboat' FAW Pauline Walsh Short Story First Prize 2017

'Coin of the Crone' FAW John Kelly Short Story Prize 2019; first published 2019 Better Read Than Dead Competition anthology *The Road Less Travelled*

'In a Circular Motion' FAW Pauline Walsh Short Story Second Prize 2012, Port Stephens Prize HC 2015, published in local press

'The Book Safe' First Prize FAW Pauline Walsh 2015; finalist Pen2Paper competition published online 2016

'No Stones' first published online *Flash Fiction Magazine* 2013

'The Patchwork Professor' FAW Pauline Walsh Short Story Second Prize 2014

'The Maid's Room' shortlisted Marjorie Barnard Award 2019

'Divertimento' FAW Pauline Walsh Short Story First Prize 2020